HOLLYWOOD TOUCH

NICOLE FRENCH

raglan

For anyone who has ever needed a safe place.

ONE

Will

"You did good, Willie. Haven't lost your touch."

I held back a smile as I stared beyond the stern of the boat, where the sun flickered across the Long Island Sound. Somewhere, a gull cried, and then another while small waves lapped against the hull. I wondered if they were some of the many that had flown with us when we'd sailed across this water yesterday.

Dad hadn't called me Willie in years. Then again, we hadn't been sailing like this in years either. Probably not since I was twenty, maybe twenty-one? The last time I'd fled New York for Stamford, the one place in the world no one gave a damn that I was Fitz Baker.

I grunted and pushed a hand through the blond hair I needed to cut. Again. The studio wasn't going to be happy.

"Be honest," I said. "You thought I was going to flip her more than once, didn't you?"

But Michael Baker wasn't the type to expand on praise. Instead, he just climbed onto the dock and grabbed the bridle to tie up the boat, leaving me to pick up the random debris scattered in the corner after five days on the water. Damn, the sun. It was hotter today than it had been all week. Unseasonably warm, even for Connecticut this time of year.

I shoved a few empty bottles into a trash bag and tried to ignore the perspiration soaking the collar of my T-shirt, then started the process of flaking the sails. Sweat poured down my forehead. Fuck, it was hot. Too hot.

Or maybe it was just me. I could admit it was a mistake to think I could go three full days without taking anything. I'd been feening since three that morning. If I didn't get a fix soon, I was going to have to throw myself in the water just to cool the fuck off.

Duffel over my shoulder, I followed my father up the dock and down the path, winding through a field of grass toward my childhood home. The little red house had been here since the twenties, according to Dad. I'd grown up with stories about the generations of family who made a life here. Passed down, fisherman to fisherman, until I spoiled it all. Before my face was discovered at a mall. Before my seven-year-old life was sold to a TV series and a soda sponsorship. Before the idea of happiness in this house was a joke.

As we reached the back porch, Dad muttered over his shoulder. What, I don't know, since at that point I was about to sprint upstairs in search of the pills calling my name from my old room. One short, rickety flight, and I'd be all right. I could do this. Mind over matter, you asshole. Mind over fucking matter.

Dad dropped the cooler on the deck and flopped into one of the Adirondack chairs facing the sound. It didn't matter that we'd literally spent five days out there. My old man would never get enough of the water.

I reached for the screen door but was stopped by a low growl.

"Will."

I turned to find Dad holding out a can of Bud.

"Sit," he ordered.

I glanced between him and the squeaky screen door. If I left now, he would know why. And it had been a good five days. Better than I'd had in a while.

I'd been holding out this long. A beer would help for another thirty minutes.

I could do it. I could.

"Thanks, Dad." I accepted the beer and sank into the chair next to him.

We sipped in silence like we had the past three nights, this time watching the twilight from home instead of whatever deserted beach we could find up and down Long Island. Dusk fell across the grasses that stretched out from the house and melted into the water.

This was what we did together. When the world was crazy, when the noise never stopped. No matter what set was calling, which cameras were flashing, which junket was scheduled...I always knew I could come here and just sit.

"Will." Dad's voice was quiet, almost lost in the breeze ruffling the overgrown grass.

But I could still hear him. "Yeah?"

"You need to stop."

My chest tightened. I didn't move my gaze from view. "Stop what?"

He didn't answer for a long time. It was a game we'd always played together. A power struggle between father and son.

Finally, I turned, and the glazed look in his eyes said exactly what he meant. I had been waiting for this for days. I knew it was coming the moment he invited me out here.

"The pills," he said. "The girls. All the trouble. It needs to stop."

Michael Baker was a gruff man. In close to twenty years, he had never once commented on the surreal life I'd been living since I booked my first major role. Longer if you counted the years I did commercial after commercial.

Okay, sure. I was no angel. Show me a former child actor who was. Hell, show me a regular actor who was. You try living clean while growing up on sets where blow is more common than sugar. Or staying innocent when you're partying at Chateau Marmont every other night. Do you have any idea how many high-priced hookers basically live at that place? I met three the first time I went. In one night. In one room. My room.

I was thirteen.

I could have been mad. I could be mad now, really. What right did he have, after years of that shit, to step in now? When his son got famous, Michael Baker just stayed here in Connecticut while Mom and I moved to the city. He let her take over my career—my entire life—while he went right on fishing, sailing, and drinking Bud like nothing had changed at all.

Part of me understood. The man was overwhelmed. How could he have known at eighteen that his high school sweetheart would turn into a fame-hungry stage mother? How could he have known that his only child would be the face on a million products, the star of the most popular television show in America, and an Oscar nominee on a thousand magazine covers?

No one plans for that. It's a sad, fucked-up lottery win.

To most of the world, all the people who knew my face but never really knew me, I was Fitz Baker, "movie star" and all-around bad apple. To my mother and a few close friends, I was Will. But to my dad, I was only Willie. Easy. Simple. Like the old days, when the most complicated thing he had to tell me was how to choose the right bait. Unlike everyone else in life, he never gave a shit about any of it. Not the fame. Not the money. None of it.

I swallowed, finding the initial wave of anger had subsided like a low tide. Michael Baker was one to let things go. He avoided confrontation like the plague. So the fact that he was saying anything at all? It mattered.

"I'm...I'm trying." I stared out at the water, avoiding the skepticism etched in thick lines across his forehead.

He didn't need to tell me things were worse. I'd been getting a metric ton of shit the last six months from my mother, my agent, my manager, my publicist, and a whole host of studio reps wanting to make sure I'd be good to go for my next projects. I asked for six months at my place in Vermont—they came back with six weeks at Betty Ford. Anything more was basically a death sentence in this business. Or so I was told.

"I know it's been hard since you and Amy split. I know." Dad drained his can, then cracked open another.

He knew it had been hard? I shook my head. He never knew. No one ever knew what that disaster of a relationship did to me.

"Sure," I said, taking my first sip. The beer had gone a little stale, slightly lukewarm after days in a cheap cooler. I fought the urge not to gulp it down. "Thanks."

"She was a pretty girl."

Fuck it. I sighed and drank long enough that I was out of breath. "That she was. Still is, actually."

"Shame you couldn't work it out."

I didn't answer. I didn't want to get into the train wreck that had been Amelia Craig and me. We had met on location when we were only twenty, and it was like one of the stupid meet-cutes in our movie. I'd walked into my trailer, and she was there, thinking it was hers. Cue hilarity. Cue fireworks. Cue a shitload of sexual tension that made for a hell of a lot of fun between takes and basically exploded before we were halfway through filming.

It was fun. And then, to my surprise, it was something more.

Amy just got it. She knew what it was like to grow up in the fishbowl with at least one overbearing parent who cared more about your next contract than your next hug. She understood what it felt like to grow up with peers a decade older than you and have to grow up well before you were ready. She was willing to listen whenever I couldn't take one more minute with my mother. She always seemed to know exactly what I needed to hear to calm down when the world was closing in.

She got it, yeah. But she also wanted to manipulate it. She wanted to be the next "Hollywood power couple," whatever that meant. And I, an idiot who thought she really loved me, went right along with it.

Pap strolls at the Grove and Santa Monica. Dinner dates at Ivy and Beso. Red carpets and promotional junkets, always hand in hand. It was still nice, having someone in the bubble with me, even if I wasn't always sure how much of Amy's affection was real and how much was for them. Her kisses in front of cameras always seemed a little more intense than the ones behind closed doors. Her smiles were always a little brighter. And when I asked her to marry me, she begged me to do it again in front of the Hollywood sign so a few of her pet photographers could snap away from behind the ragweed bushes.

I loved her, though. Or I thought I did. And the press and public ate it the fuck up.

But not as much as they chowed down on our breakup.

To me, it was a simple split. We got along until we didn't. The months apart, with separate filming and promotional schedules—that would be enough to get to anyone, wouldn't it? Phone calls stopped. Texting stopped. It was clear to me, as it was to her, that we didn't have what it took to keep things going in the long run. Not in this business. Not as young as we were.

So, there were tears, yeah. A few shouting matches, maybe, on both sides. And finally, a midnight conversation that lasted until the sun came up. But by the end, we agreed together that we were better off apart. We'd wait a few more months to announce it quietly once our existing promotional work was done. Things got crazy enough during a blitz without relationship drama to bait people. We had a plan. Keep things professional and private.

Two weeks later, pictures started to appear in the papers. On the tabloids sites. Pictures of me and another actress, Patti Court. And, of course, headlines to match.

Patti cake, Patti cake, Baker's *girl*?

Fitz Baker puts his thumb in multiple pies!

Fitz Flies with Fresh Fling!

Fitz cheats!—and Amelia's Broken Heart.

It was all lies. Every fucking word. I didn't know Patti

Court from Adam, but somehow, she kept showing up at my events. Sitting next to me at the Chateau. Slipping her fingers into mine at just the right second.

Did she kiss me? Apparently. I honestly don't remember what went down, although that was nothing new. But Amy and I had been done for weeks before those photos were taken. I didn't cheat. I might be guilty of a lot of things, but cheating is not and never would be one of them.

I might have made it if it hadn't been for that. No reason a breakup had to break *me* too.

Then, a month later, Amy's next movie broke box office records while mine tanked. A week after that, a stalker broke into my house in Malibu and attacked me with a knife. I was rushed to the hospital, coked out of my mind and bleeding out of my side. The media had a field day. The paparazzi camped outside my house went from five to thirty overnight.

The occasional panic attacks that had started years before got even worse, and therefore, so did my reliance on whatever could take them away. I was scared of my own shadow the second I got out of the hospital. Two months later, I still was.

Benzos helped. Other stuff too. I wasn't exactly picky.

A speedboat blared past the edge of the dock, and automatically, I yanked up my collar and lowered the bill of my hat to hide my face, despite the fact that it was a good fifty yards off.

No one had found me yet on this trip. But they would. They always did.

My stomach clenched—that familiar gnawing. The first sign another attack was imminent. I sighed and rubbed my thumb around the rim of my beer can. The pills upstairs were calling.

No one should feel this old at almost twenty-five.

"I'm trying," I told Dad again. "I went to Killington, didn't I?"

After getting out of the hospital, I escaped to the retreat I bought in Vermont. It's huge—an old farm on the side of a mountain. I saw it when I was on location and fell in love with the peace and quiet of it. The way the woods swallowed everything up, including me. Nothing's better than solitude after having your broken heart splashed everywhere for the world to devour.

Then the neighbors tagged me, and the paps figured out where I was. And then work called. Life called. And it was easier just to take a shot. Swallow a pill. Live in my haze and deal with it.

"What if I just moved back here for a while?" I ventured. "The neighbors wouldn't care. They know me. They don't bother me." I tipped my head toward the street, toward the bouncing sounds of kids playing Horse. Mrs. Murphy shouted at them over her azaleas. It was so...normal.

Or at least, what I thought normal sounded like.

Dad emitted a loud snort. "You think your mother is going to be all right with that?"

"She's not my manager anymore."

"Tell her that."

I ignored him. Six years after I fired her and switched to Benny Amaya, my current manager and best friend, Mom was still doing everything she could to wedge her foot back in that particular door. We hadn't spoken at all for nearly two months after I did it. But there was the deal with Del Conte to contend with, the one that had made me fire her to begin with. I was seventeen and wanted out of the entertainment industry so I could attend Brown. Instead, my mother signed my life away for a four-picture deal with Del Conte Entertainment.

I had three down. One to promote. One more to film.

And she'd be there to make sure I did every minute of that work so she could get every dollar of her commission.

"You managed to get away this week," Dad said. "But what's going to happen when she figures out where you are? Or when the damn photographers do? What would happen to them?"

With a tip of his head toward the kids' laughter in the background, he showed whose safety he was concerned about. It wasn't mine.

I imagined the homely North Stamford neighborhood overrun with photogs. I saw the kids forced inside so they wouldn't be stampeded by the crazy fan girls. I felt the anger and frustration emitting from faces that had only ever looked at me as friends before.

It wouldn't take long, and they would ask me to leave. Everyone wants to be next to a star for a minute. No one wants more than a day.

Maybe Benny was right. Maybe the best option was to stop trying to escape the madness of the city and just embrace the fishbowl for what it was. Buy an apartment in New York—a penthouse with twenty-four-hour security, above the range of the telephotos across the street. The kind of place where, even if they could see me come and go, at least I could see them, too.

My heart picked up a few beats, and a steel band wrapped around my chest along with the clenching in my gut. I closed my eyes and tried to breathe. But I couldn't.

There was just no space. Not even on the boat. Or on this porch. There was no space in this world for me.

I drained the rest of my beer and reached for another,

then shotgunned half of it before Dad could say a word. The front door to the house creaked, audible even where we were sitting.

"Dad," I said. "You really need to oil those hinges."

Dad shrugged. "You gonna do it, Willie? How many six-packs would you need for that to happen?"

He was just giving me shit, but the hint of contempt still sliced.

"I could do it," I said, then shotgunned the rest of the second beer. Twenty-four ounces in less than a minute. And that wasn't even close to my record.

But before I grabbed a third, Dad snagged the last can and set it by his side with a covert glance my way. The bottle of pills in my old room was shouting now. Screaming. I just needed one to take the edge off. One to lighten the thousand-pound load on my shoulders and loosen the lasso around my waist.

"I'm just going to go to the bath—"

A clip-clop of heels on the battered oak interrupted my bullshit excuse.

Dad and I both twisted in our chairs as Tricia Owens-Baker stepped onto the deck, wrinkling her long nose at the salty smell of the shore.

TWO

Will

There she was. Someone who used to be my mother. Now she was just another bloodsucking leech with bottle-blond hair who wore tailored Michael Kors and too many gems to count.

"There you are! Will, what are you doing here?" she demanded without preamble. "You're supposed to be in the city at five. You have a photocall."

Tricia Owens-Baker checked her watch, a diamond-encrusted Bulgari she was gifted for a spot I did for them maybe eight years ago. She loved that watch, even though she had ten others that were more ostentatious. That year was when she started taking on clients besides me, and she met her first one at that shoot.

Had she always been this way? I didn't know. For as far back as I could remember, she had scheduled commercial spots instead of doctor's appointments. Taken me to auditions instead of Little League games.

"It's almost four," she blustered. "Look at you. You look

like you've been in the water for a week and laid out to dry for another. Have you even shaved? Your stylist is going to eat you for breakfast. The people from Dolce are at the hotel now about to walk, and you know how hard Benny —and I—worked to get you that sponsorship, Will. This isn't just about you!"

I grimaced. Fashion spots were the worst. I never asked to dress like a fucking Jetsons character while thousands of cameras flashed at me, but apparently, that's what happens when you reach a certain level of fame. The last time I walked a red carpet, the designers put me in a harness. Like I was about to go zip lining. Took me ten minutes just to get out of it so I could take a piss.

"Trish, leave the boy alone. We just got in."

"He's not a boy anymore, *Michael*. And I can't leave him alone because his *manager*"—resentment lathered the word—"won't stop calling, asking me where he is. I'm not even getting paid for this anymore, Fitzwilliam. Lord, help me understand why I keep doing it."

Because you're a greedy control freak who can't deal with her biggest meal ticket turning her away?

I just stared out at the water, putting everything I had into not tapping my foot and fidgeting with my fingers— dead giveaways that both my parents knew well. Ten minutes. I could give her ten minutes without tipping her off.

Be present. That's what the shrinks always told me to do. Identify with things in my immediate present to ground me.

Focus on the sky. It was turning orange here and there with the setting sun, a deep purple hue rising above the clouds. The catamaran bobbed up and down, the mast spearing the clouds. For a moment, I imagined myself running off the porch and sailing away. It wouldn't take much. I could hop on, cut the lines, and go. Leave this all behind.

"Fitzwilliam! Are you even listening to me?

I sighed. "Not really."

Better to be harsh. Better so she'd know for sure that I was never hiring her back. And she would never forgive me for it. Or stop trying to weasel her way back in.

Mom chucked my cell phone, which I had left in the house, into my lap with unnecessary force. "Check your messages, Will. I told you, you're in trouble."

I scowled at the screen. Fourteen missed calls. Ten missed messages. Okay, so maybe I should have told Benny I was skipping the photocall. It wasn't a major event—they usually let the supporting actors do them alone since the other headliners and I would be stuck in junket interviews from about six a.m. to midnight tomorrow.

And then there was the premiere on Friday. A thousand screaming fans. Flashes so bright you can't see for hours after. Tipped paparazzi trailing you to every club, gym, or convenience store you might visit in between. Then do it all over again in a new city. And another. And another. Rinse and repeat for six weeks.

The thought made me shake. My right-hand fingers started to tap out the rhythm of Alice In Chains' "Nutshell" on my knee. The pills were screaming.

Dad patted my knee. "Better get a move on, Will. You made a commitment. "

And that, if anything, was my dad's entire motto. It was the reason he let Mom truck me to every set between here and Miami for years. It was why he would take the boat out in a windstorm if he promised to, why he stayed married to a woman he hadn't lived with in almost twenty years.

A man does what he says he's going to do. No matter what.

I crushed my empty cans underfoot, then stood. I was anything but photocall-ready in an old pair of paint-smeared jeans, a Utah Jazz T-shirt that I'd borrowed from an assistant, and beat-up Chucks that Amelia had hated. My hair, blond like my mother's, was a messy mop over my ears. Mom was right. I hadn't shaved in over a week either.

Both my stylist and my trainer were probably the authors of at least four of those messages, wondering where the hell I was. It was time to go back to real life, which ironically was a life less real than anything.

"Thanks for the sail, Dad." I clapped him on the shoulder. "I'll see you next time I'm in town."

"When's that?"

Mentally, I went over the next month, or what I remembered of the schedule. Honestly, it was Benny who kept track of these things, not me.

"New York and LA for the talk show circuits. Then Cannes, Paris, London, and Buenos Aires," Mom cut in.

I sighed. She still knew my schedule better than anyone, and sometimes that came in handy. Maybe we could arrange an assistant position if she really wanted it that badly.

"After that, you've got the Hong Kong, Tokyo, and Sydney premieres," she continued. "Two days home in LA before you're off to Atlanta for the next shoot."

With every city, my shoulders drooped. More hotels. More chaos. More feeling like a rat trapped in a never-ending maze.

"Right." I fished my keys out of my pocket. "I should get going, then."

"Will, you can't possibly be driving," Mom said. "We *barely* got you out of that second DUI last year."

"I've had two shitty beers," I countered. "I'm *fine*."

"The studio is covered with paparazzi. I saw them myself."

"And did you call them yourself too?"

My mother opened and closed her pink-painted lips like a fish. That's all I needed to know. Any generous thoughts about being my assistant floated right off with the breeze.

"Got it," I snapped. "I said I'll drive myself. The press can fuck off, and that's it."

"Just leave him, Trish," Dad said as Mom tried to protest. "He's got to do things on his own."

That was about the best endorsement I could ever hope to get from the guy.

I twirled the keys to Benny's Bentley. "I'll just get my stuff from upstairs and head out."

Both of my parents, one sitting, one standing, watched me leave. Neither made a move to hug me. Neither wished me a safe journey.

"Thanks again for the trip, Dad," I said. "I needed it."

My father's gray eyes softened, and the stern lines over his forehead dissipated. "Take care of yourself, Willie."

I nodded. I could have said I'd try...but that would have been a damn lie.

THREE

Maggie

"Stand up. Let me get a look at you."

Calliope Jackson, my best friend and brand-new manager, stood in the dressing room in a pair of sleek leather pants, a bright red crop top that showed off her impressive abs, and a pair of big hoop earrings that reached her shoulders. She looked a lot more stage-ready than me, the actual talent.

Holy crap. A *dressing room*. Not some graffiti-riddled supply closet at a dingy Brooklyn bar. This room had lights. A makeup table. Even a chair behind the screen to change. Amenities for talent—something I'd always wanted to call myself but never thought I would. At least, not at twenty-two. Not with another month left of college. Not with literally five dollars and forty-two cents in my bank account.

But it seemed my fortunes were finally changing. Four years ago, I left my tiny hometown in Eastern Washington for the Big Apple, armed with a scholarship, my guitar, and a dream to be a songwriter. I'd expected to take ten years or longer to work my way into a venue like Irving Plaza. Instead, with Calliope's help, my ship was coming in a little earlier than expected. Or, you know, whatever else you'd call something like a show that was potentially my big break.

I stood up next to Callie and we peered into the mirror over the dressing table. I wasn't due to go on for several hours, but I was nervous. The club owner had let us in early before sound check, and Calliope was taking advantage of the fact that I was finally letting her style me. We'd already tried out two dresses and two other hairstyles with them— this on top of the forty other outfits my friend had submitted out of her closet.

I'd vetoed everything. A Diana Ross-esque comb-out didn't look much like a folk singer to me. Nor did a bright gold dress or sky-high heels. How was I supposed to play a guitar in front of thousands while teetering on pins?

"I think this is it." Callie picked up one of my natural spirals, which had been restructured with a curling iron, and set it back over my shoulder.

Her hand floated over the glossy curls. When I moved to New York, Callie—then simply my roommate—had taken it upon herself to fix my hair "situation," as she called it. It didn't matter that I'd grown up the daughter of a hair-dresser. Mama didn't know anything about women who looked like Callie and me. My curls weren't as tight as my friend's, but they were still solidly corkscrew ringlets, likely passed on, along with my slightly darker skin and black-brown eyes, from the father I had never known. In my hometown, I was the only person for miles with hair like mine—whatever that meant.

Don't, I thought. This night, of all nights, I couldn't fall into my usual sinkhole of doubt. I had come to New York to get away from the things that were my only legacy back home. Maggie Sharp, the kid with no father. Maggie, the daughter of the town drunk.

It had taken me four years in this city to become Maggie Sharp, accomplished musician. But the doubt still seeped through.

"I don't know," I said, picking up the thick curl. "I still feel like I don't look country enough for this crowd."

Another thing I'd been telling myself since always. Sure, I grew up on country, listening to Loretta Lynn and Patsy Cline on my mother's stereo. I taught myself to pick out the basic pattern of "Folsom Prison" on a friend's guitar before I entered grade school. Though it wasn't the only kind of music I wrote now, after spending four years on a music scholarship at NYU, country was where my roots were, and my older songs were what got me this gig tonight.

But none of those singers looked like me.

Maggie Sharp, musician. If I could just remember that, I'd be fine.

Calliope rolled her eyes and put the curl back. "Don't go there, babe. Not tonight. No one in that audience is going to question your bona fides once you start crooning. I promise."

I looked at my friend, who was and always would be unapologetically her beautiful, queenly self. Rooming with Callie had been a revelation, and now that she was my manager, I hoped her self-confidence would continue to rub off. Especially tonight.

Two weeks ago, Calliope answered a call from someone looking for a last-minute replacement opener for folk singer Gillian Jacobs. When she sent them my tape instead of forwarding them to her boss, it was a risk that could have cost Callie her job. Instead, she was promoted from intern to talent rep. One signature later, I became her first official client right after I finished my last midterm.

So really, it was *our* big break.

I went back to studying my hair, picking up a few tendrils, pulling them over my shoulder, then to the back, then flopping them forward again.

"Babe. *Stop.* You look fine, and there is still time to fix things. We settled on the blue dress, right?"

I glanced at her through the mirror. "Yes, that's definitely the one."

Callie was lending me a cerulean off-the-shoulder dress with a short, flouncy skirt and a long ruffle across the chest. It was a shorter, sexier version of an outfit June Carter famously wore on one of her tours with Johnny Cash. It made my skin glow.

"Good," Callie said. "You've got soundcheck in a few, so it's probably time to get out there. The band is already here, and Bill, the club manager, is kind of a stickler for schedules."

I grabbed my guitar case off the couch, my heart rattling in my chest. This was the hardest part. I wasn't a natural performer—never had been. But I was told time and time again that if I wanted to sell my songs, playing them myself was the only way to do it.

"All right," I said. "Let's go."

THE HOUSE BAND was a group of veteran musicians who mostly earned their money backing bigger artists in the studio. Both guitarists were over fifty, and the drummer was probably closer to sixty-five, but we had only needed to practice twice for them to learn my songs, almost better than I knew them. Ray, George, and Andrew were some of the best I'd ever worked with. Just one more way tonight was my winning lottery ticket.

"All right," called Kate, the sound tech, from a booth at the far end of the venue.

It was three o'clock. The show wouldn't start for another six hours. But this was the time for every act to practice their songs with the exact right sound levels. I'd run through a few bars of each, let the tech adjust, and have the afternoon free.

"Hey, Maggie," Ray, the bassist, greeted me as I walked onstage. "Ready, kiddo?"

"I think so."

I set my guitars on the stands next to the center mic. I had two for the show—my Martin in standard tuning and my Ovation in open D. My most prized possessions. Each instrument had cost me nearly three months of rent in exchange for just about every other luxury I could think of. I didn't have a computer, much less a smartphone or even regular internet access. I never went out with friends, hadn't even seen a movie in close to four years. I shared a two-bedroom apartment with three other struggling artists. Music was my life, and these guitars were its oxygen. Nothing else mattered.

"Everyone have the set list?" I looked at the other band members. We'd determined the order of songs yesterday during our final practice at a studio space in Queens, but there was always a chance someone had forgotten it.

Everyone nodded. George, the drummer, waved his scrap of paper above the cymbals.

I turned to the sound booth. "Kate, should we..."

"Ready when you are."

The venue was fully lit, the black seats and painted

walls grayish under the harsh fluorescent lights. It wasn't intimidating right now when you could see everyone's worry lines and the sneaker marks on the floor. But tonight, when the room was jam-packed and the giant spotlights hanging from the ceiling were pointed straight at me? Well, let's just say failure really wasn't an option.

I turned around and nodded at George to count us off for the first song, "Blue Jay."

He tapped his sticks together. "A-one, two, three, *four*."

Like they had been playing it for years, the band launched into the song I'd written at sixteen while I watched a blue jay hop around the snow after a blizzard. It was a song about loneliness, about being scared of the world. It was a song about taking chances anyway.

We finished the fourth bar of the intro. I stepped up to the mic, opened my mouth...and screwed everything up.

Oh, they call you a careful dreamer—

The notes came out raw, timid, and, worst of all, completely off pitch. I winced while the boys kept playing, then stepped up to sing again. This time I went sharp. Badly.

I was mortified.

I had perfect pitch. I could hear a flat A miles away. I knew even now that Andrew needed to tune his D string slightly higher. I had played this song perfectly at countless bars around the city.

So what was going on?

George counted us off, and we launched back into the intro. Once again, I stepped up to the mic.

Oh, they call you a careful dreamer—

Before that last word came out, the band had stopped completely. In the booth, Kate was shaking her head, probably wondering who invited College Open Mic night to Gillian's show. I looked to the side of the stage, where Calliope was watching with an uncharacteristically worried expression.

I turned back to the band. "Why did you stop?"

The three older men looked at each other awkwardly, but it was Ray who spoke up.

"Maggie, look. You're nervous. We get it. But you can do better than that. You need a shot, kid? Something to loosen up?" He gestured toward his denim vest pocket, where I could see the outline of a small flask.

I swallowed. It was tempting. It really was. But I had sworn long ago I was *never* going to turn into my mother. Not even one shot's worth.

"No, I don't think so. I'll be okay."

I turned back to the mic and promptly stumbled on a crack in the stage. I came down on my other foot with a loud smack so hard my guitar strings twanged along with it.

Andrew rubbed his forehead while muttering something like, "Christ."

"I'm fine," I said. "Just give me a second."

Ray grimaced, though not without kindness. "This is Irving Plaza, hon. You can't start your set sounding like a...a..."

"Like a high school musical audition," Andrew supplied without looking up from his bass.

I frowned at him. "What's that supposed to mean?"

The older man sighed, then wiggled his mustache. "Maggie, I don't know you very well, but I know one thing—you've got talent. We wouldn't have agreed to play this show if you didn't."

I swallowed.

Ray continued. "Kiddo, this is *your* show tonight. These are *your* songs. So you got to take charge from the second you step on this stage. If you hear that George is offbeat—"

"Hey, now," George piped up from the back.

"—and George, you know you were," Ray continued, though he looked straight at me. "You have to say something. I saw you wince when Andrew chimed in. Something you want to tell him?"

I glanced nervously at Andrew. The bassist had a heavily lined face and facial hair that hid most of his expressions. He didn't blink, daring me to say something.

"Ah—" I cleared my throat awkwardly. *Get it together, Maggie.* "Yeah. Okay. Andrew, your D-string is flat."

His mouth dropped. "It is not—"

"It is," I said with a surety that had Ray nodding. "And George, you *were* late, and it screwed me up even more than my nerves did." I turned to Kate and stepped up to the mic. This time, my voice didn't falter. "Can I get a little more on bass, please?"

For that, I received a thumbs-up from the sound booth.

I turned back to the band. "Okay, boys, let's try it again."

FOUR

Will

"Next week, Pop? Before I have to leave?"

As he walked us out to the driveway, Dad ignored my question. Probably because we both knew the answer. I wasn't coming back anytime soon, because once I jumped back in the rat race, no one was letting me out until I crossed every finish line and won them all a good pot. That was me. A prize-winning rat.

The skin at the corners of Dad's eyes crinkled as he examined Mom's car, a sleek Mercedes coup worth more than most of the houses on this street. "What happened to the old one?"

Tricia let out a very unladylike snort. "Michael, please. I can't cart clients around in a five-year-old car. What would they think of me?"

"How about that you're halfway frugal? That car was barely two years old."

Mom scowled. The way she spent money had been an

issue since I could remember. I honestly wasn't sure why he even bothered at this point.

Actually, that's not true. I knew exactly why he was pushing her buttons. It was his way of hanging on to the remnants of the life we all used to share. Deep down, he probably even still loved her. I had never actually seen my parents show affection, but I noticed how he watched her when she was around. Tricia Owens was Michael Baker's polar opposite—full of life and chatter while he was stolid and soft-spoken. They met at a high school party, where Mom was singing karaoke—so they said. It wasn't hard to imagine. Mom had a thing for Pat Benatar and a half-decent voice. The green-eyed, golden-haired girl had caught the eye of a fisherman's kid, whom she'd dragged to the living room-turned-dance floor and hooked like a striped bass.

"Come on," I said. "Dad, if you're really that worried, I gave Mom the down payment. Mom, let's go."

"Yes, let's. But Fitzwilliam, *I* am driving. What would Benny say if you crashed his Bentley?"

She had a point there. Benny was my best friend, but he loved his car above all else.

I glanced ruefully at the Bentley flashing in front of us. Or maybe that was just the pill I took starting to kick in. If she was distracted enough, maybe I could sneak another before we reached the hotel.

"Fine, fine," I said. "Let's just go."

Mom put on her sunglasses, gold rims blinking like stars in the afternoon sun. "Michael."

"Trish."

So much for a lovers' goodbye.

Dad lumbered back to the house, pausing by the door to watch us leave. I raised a hand toward my father. He watched me for a long minute, like he wanted to say something. But when he lifted his beer can in response, his weathered face didn't move.

THE CONNECTICUT COUNTRYSIDE was gradually giving way to sound barriers and telephone wires. After arranging pickup for Benny's car, Mom was taking back-to-back calls from other clients. I just let the scenery blur along with her voice.

Forty-five minutes. I had forty-five minutes before I was back in the city. In the old days, I'd sneak around back of wherever we were headed. Call ahead to find out where the alley or parking entrance to the hotel, venue, or even restaurant was. As long as my mother wasn't there, I had a fighting chance.

Tricia Owens-Baker never missed a publicity opportunity. No doubt she'd notified the paps on her way here if the studio hadn't already. By now, there would be at least a dozen of them outside the hotel, along with fans and more than a few reporters. The official press would be ushered to the roof, where the studio was holding the photocall before the premiere tomorrow night. Once that was done, I'd have interviews until about eight. After that, more schmoozing. Dinner with the executives. Critics. More kissing the ass of every bigwig they could get to come to this thing.

It all started in forty-five minutes. I just had to sit here and be cool.

I turned and caught my reflection in the side-view mirror. Mom was right. I looked like shit. Tired and strung out, too thin for my own good. It looked all right in pictures. Everyone wants cheekbones and a cut jaw. But in person, I was a shadow, gray-skinned and sweaty. Barely recognizable as *People* magazine's "Sexiest Man Alive."

What a crock of shit.

"What are you doing?" my mother asked as I twisted around to the back.

"Looking for something."

"Looking for what? Will, I am trying to drive. Turn around."

"I have a headache."

I located my jacket and sat back down while I fished in the pocket. I was pretty sure I'd left a baggie in there with some Demerol I'd picked up at an industry party last week. The other pill wasn't doing shit, and after my Valium ran out, my shrink wasn't willing to write me another scrip until the end of the month. Something about "risk of addiction."

It was severe agoraphobia combined with a panic disorder. They suspected as much when I was young and would throw up in a bush after almost every red carpet, but I wasn't formally diagnosed until I was thirteen. That was after the Emmys. After, according to the tabloids, I stopped being that cute kid from *Bailey's Life,* and turned into a full-fledged "heartthrob." Hey, those were the words of *US Weekly*, not me.

Just the term made my entire chest squeeze and my stomach turn. People were fucking crazy. Hordes of teenage girls started following me everywhere, and a pretty sizable number of their mothers and fathers too. The more I tried to ignore them, the more they seemed to crave my attention. Craved anything about me while not knowing me at all.

For a while, Amelia made it better. There were two of us in the fishbowl, so even if we couldn't escape it, I thought maybe we could distract each other with enough sex and affection that we could ignore our rabid audience. Pretend —*act*—like we were alone.

And God, did she ever. She even fooled me.

I slam my head back against the seat. Thinking about Amy was *not* going to help me get through this evening. Neither was thinking about that asshole and his knife. Fucking hell, where did I put those other pills? Did I take the last one yesterday when we were at the beach?

I didn't usually like taking opiates if I could help it. This was why.

I clapped a hand against my jeans pocket. Empty too.

"Fuck. *Fuck.*"

I yanked the half-empty box of cigarettes out of my other pocket, found my Zippo, and lit up. The smoke curled inside my chest, taking off the edge, but not much more than that.

"Gina, I have to go." Mom cut off whatever industry hack she was chatting to and scowled at me. "Will, what is wrong with you today? Why are you so edgy? Shouldn't this little trip with your father have helped with that?"

I blew out a long stream of smoke and scowled. "It did. And now it's over."

"Seems like it made things even worse. You know I don't allow smoking in my car, Fitzwilliam."

Her voice was somehow even shriller than normal, cutting through me like a knife, stabbing into my chest.

I rolled down the window and blew a lungful of smoke into the sunlight. "Do you want me to fucking go to this thing or not, *Tricia?*"

She had the sense to cringe—she knew I only used her given name as a warning. She knew if she didn't stop push-ing, I was liable to do something nuts. Like jump out of a moving car or force the wheel.

"Will..."

"Look," I continued. "If you want to get behind security to spread your card around like the clap, you'll need me in one piece to do it. Right now, that requires nicotine. Can you deal with that for twenty minutes?"

She worried her mouth a bit, but for once, she didn't reply. I didn't even bother hating the fact that my mother had cared more about her own business than anything else for years. More than her own marriage. Certainly more than her son.

My fingers twitched on my knee. Jesus *Christ*, I needed something else. Like right fucking *now*.

New York spilled into the sky, its skyscrapers crawling up the horizon like goblin shadows. Or maybe the edges of a fortress. Or a cage.

The cigarettes went fast. Too fast. I took a final drag off the last and tossed it out the window. Careless, of course. A cigarette could cause a brush fire. But I honestly didn't give a shit if this entire city burned to the fucking ground.

Maybe it should.

And me with it.

The pound of the wheels on pavement.

The grind of car gears.

The click-click of the blinker.

Everything was louder. The sky brighter. My head pounded like someone was slamming an anvil on it.

Benny really needed to have the hookup when I got to the hotel. He knew me too well not to.

"Do you have any Tylenol?" I demanded. "How about Excedrin? *Anything*? What's in here?"

Without waiting for her to answer, I rooted through the glove compartment of her car.

"Will, there's nothing in there besides the registration

and a manual." She kept her polished fingers at a perfect ten and two.

"What about this?" Beneath two pairs of gloves (my mother would be the one person who actually keeps gloves in a glove compartment), I spotted the telltale orange of a prescription bottle peeking out of a makeup bag. Jackpot.

"That? Will, you don't want that. I don't even know why that's in there. It's expired, probably from when I had that cyst removed two years ago."

I opened the bottle and shook out two pills. Without water, they stuck to my throat, scratching as they went down, but I didn't care. Percocet works fast, and I had less than thirty minutes until flashes and fans.

"It's good enough," I mumbled as a familiar, welcome haze descended. "Just drive."

I ignored the pity overlaying my mother's selfish gaze. I didn't want it. The city approached in the distance, its spindly jaws open, waiting to swallow me whole. Waiting for the moment when I no longer cared if it did.

FIVE

Will

By the time we finally reached Manhattan, every sharp edge was a blur. The world was hazy again. Not exactly pleasant. More like a blanket that might suffocate. Still, shelter is shelter, and that's all I wanted. Christ. Expired or not, those pills *worked*.

"Let me out here."

I gestured toward the hotel, a mottled mass of brick and bronze towering over Fifth Avenue like an ancient deity. That was New York for you. Swagger and stone. God, I hated this city.

"Will, you don't want to get out now. The paparazzi are clearly here, waiting for the junket to start, and Benny *still* hasn't sent down security."

My mother's voice dripped with contempt, the words seeping into my ears like molasses. She always loved when she could point out Benny's deficiencies. Honestly, she loved pointing out *anyone*'s deficiencies. As if she could do any better. If she were in charge, sure, maybe there would have been six hulking guards there to walk me into the building. But they wouldn't be there to protect me. Fuck no. Their presence would call attention to the prize, letting everyone know that *Fitz Baker* was in transit from one cage to another.

Because that was all I really was to any of them. A trapped animal. Their golden calf. A pathetic cash cow.

Fuuuucccckkkk thaaaatttt. The words yawned inside my head.

I yanked on the door handle, tripping over the lock. "I said let me out." I fumbled with the latch, then tried again.

"Will! The car is still moving!"

"Then you better stop it so I don't mess up my pretty face before photos."

Just like with the cigarettes, she gave in. Because some publicity *is* bad—especially the kind where your movie star son rolls out of a car into moving traffic, and you're at the wheel.

Maybe I wished, just a little, that she would keep going. As far back as I could remember, a part of me wanted her to be the type of mother who, whether I was five or twenty-five, would pull the car over to the side of the road on *her* choice, not mine, and let me have it. Who wouldn't let me get away with my shit. Instead, she let me do what I wanted as long as I performed on time. She gave in, not to be generous or to protect me from getting hurt, but to guard her own fucking interests.

The Benz veered gently to the curb and I got out, ignoring her huffs.

"Thanks for the ride."

Before she could answer, I slammed the door and

swayed toward the hotel entrance. And immediately, I was swarmed. Fuck. Oh, *fuck*.

"Fitz!"

"It's Fitz Baker!"

"Fitz, over here!"

"Where's Patti, Fitz?"

"Are you tired of her yet?"

"Are you high?"

"What does Amelia think of Patti?"

"Is Amelia dating Clark Lyman?"

I clapped a hand over my breast pocket, only to find I had forgotten the single most important part of my grand entrance: sunglasses. The world was a shitty watercolor painting—the burgundy of the doorman's coat blended right in with the brick exterior; the brass trimming was one-dimensional with the gleam of the windowpanes. And even in the sunlight, the dozens of flashes currently going off would make me see stars for the next two hours.

"Off," I snapped at one photographer, shoving him roughly away.

But it was like gray hairs, or so the girls in makeup liked to say. Pull out one, and five more come back? You push one photographer, ten more in your face.

"Fitz!"

"Why did you push him, Fitz?"

"Are you angry about Amelia's premiere?"

"Oh my *God*, that's Fitz Baker?"

I couldn't even tell them apart—the invasive questions, the hands on my clothes. Were those girls squealing or cars stopping? Photographers or fans? I shouldn't have gotten out. My heart was beating a mile a fucking minute, but my head felt like everything was working in slow-motion. My hands flailed in front of me as I stumbled toward the revolving glass doors.

"Welcome, Mr. Baker," the faceless doorman greeted me.

"Fitz!" cried the voices, bodies, and succubi behind me.

Not one of them really knew my name. Sometimes I wondered if anyone ever did.

"Fuck! Jesus, Will, what the fuck are you doing out here?"

My arm was grabbed, and I was yanked through the crowd, only registering inside that it was Benny Amaya, my manager and, I supposed, the best friend I had.

"Ben." My voice was hoarse. The world kept spinning. I just wanted to go to sleep while the pills in my jacket pocket rattled.

"Let him through, guys, all right?" Benny ordered in his familiar singsong Bronx accent. He wasn't rude. Benny had an edge, but he always got along with the paps. He liked them, and they liked him.

Not me, though. Not fucking at all.

"What's wrong with Fitz, Benny?"

"Is he ready for the premiere?"

"Is Amelia coming tonight?"

"We gotta get ready, guys. Just let us through, all right?"

The flashes didn't stop, and neither did the questions. But the bodies did let off as Benny guided me into the hotel. A prickly, tingling sensation trailed in their absence. How fucked up was it that the people who touched me most in this world were strangers? What in the *fuck* was that?

Benny released my arm, and I stumbled after him, ignoring the curious looks from the concierge, the front desk, and the bellhops.

Fuck 'em. Fuck *all* the bloodsucking onlookers.

"Easy, tiger," Ben said, and it was only then I realized I had spoken aloud. "Come on. Lila is here from Dolce to get you ready."

The elevator closed us in, and my eyes closed too. God, I needed to sleep.

"Will? Will!"

A quick slap across my face woke me up.

I started, then scowled. "Christ, Ben."

"You can't pass out right now. Jesus, what did you take?"

I pulled the bottle out of my pocket and shook it in front of Benny's face like a maraca. I cackled. The weirdest things made me laugh when I was high. I was willing to take what little humor I could find.

Benny snatched the bottle. "Goddammit." He swore again in Spanish. "Trish knows better than to give you this shit. *You* know better than this." He looked up, black eyes sparking. "One week, asshole. I just needed you to deal for *one more week*, and then we get you into rehab. You promised."

"I didn't promise shit," I slurred as the elevator doors opened. "Plus, we got the tour. M-mommy dearest said."

"Mommy ain't your manager, boyo. I am. And the studio will forgive a few weeks as long as you're sober for the LA premiere."

I followed him down a long hall and into a hotel room marked "The Presidential Suite." I snorted. Fucking nothing presidential about me.

"Yo, what do you need to wake up right now, Will? Pills? Girls? Both? What?"

Benny checked his watch while I collapsed on the couch, giggling to myself.

"Shit." Benny rubbed his forehead. "We got an hour

until photocall, and I need you coherent, all right? That shit you took in the car, no more of that. You need an upper?"

Drearily, I nodded. My head felt like it might roll off. "Or a nap."

"No. *No naps*, Will. Lila's about to dress you, and then you've got the photocall up top, plus about five interviews, and then we have that show at Irving Plaza. I know you, brother. You fall asleep now, we won't be talking until three a.m." He strode to a duffel bag in the back of the room and haphazardly fished through a few small baggies. "Goddammit. Where the fuck are those?"

"Damn, Ben. You running a pharmacy over there or something?"

I cackled again at my own joke. Benny hated doing this for me, but he also knew better than to let me try another press call sober.

"Motherfucker, you *know* I don't do this shit. This here is for you until we can get your ass into rehab where you belong." He pulled out a bag of small white pills and turned toward me. "How many did you take? Two? Three?"

I nod.

"Will!"

"Two. I took two." My voice croaked. I needed water. "Plus two beers at the house. And a benzo. I think."

Benny swore again as he shook a pill into his palm. "Take this. But nothing else, you got me? *Nothing else*, you crazy asshole. I'm not taking you to the hospital again."

With a grateful nod, I swallowed the pill. This was my life—a fucking seesaw. Uppers and downers. Cages and fishbowls.

I just wanted to get off the damn ride, but I didn't know how.

A knock at the door broke through my musing. Benny zipped up the duffel and handed me a bottle of water.

"Drink it. All of it."

With a sharp look that said I should *not* cross him, he went to answer the door.

"Sit up, Will," he ordered as he let in the team of stylists. "Time to turn you into Fitz Baker."

SIX

Maggie

"**B**enny, why in the fuck are we doing a second photocall? At a concert, of all things?"

I swiped a dry cloth over the body of my guitar as a harsh male voice filtered up from downstairs. The dressing rooms had been taken over by some of the other bands while the venue was getting ready for tonight. I was sitting alone in one of the balconies that would eventually be the VIP section, polishing and re-polishing my guitars and watching the other acts as they went through their soundchecks.

The boys had told me I was nuts, that I should leave for the few hours and get some lunch with Calliope. Instead, I ate leftover curry in the dressing room and then moved upstairs, content for a bit of solitude. New York could be crazy sometimes, and this part of the club was actually peaceful right now. Just what I hoped was needed to get my head right.

"I swear to God, man." Another male voice answered the first. "I have told you this about four times. Gillian did the entire soundtrack for *Fury*. She comes to the premiere, we show up for the tour. The tour where she will be playing almost every song on *your fuckin' movie* to the world. Two photocalls. Two press tours. One big splash. That's the contract."

"Hey." Calliope collapsed beside me. "How's it going?"

I grinned, but before I could answer, the first voice made a sharp retort. "One big splash? Am I fucking Nemo? I guess that makes you Dory, Ben." He broke into a sudden staccato laugh that seemed cut with bitterness more than joy.

"You're a fuckin' asshole, is what you are."

Calliope snorted slightly. I just rolled my eyes.

"Why? Is Amy going to make another surprise appearance? I still think you knew she was going to be at that photocall."

"Will, for the tenth damn time, *I did not know*. That was all Tricia's doing, man. Not mine."

"So she's not going to be here tonight?"

"Not if I have anything to say about it. Now, come on, man. We need to clean you up again."

"Who is that?" I mouthed as the voices left the room.

"I'd guess Benny Amaya," Calliope replied. "He mostly manages actors. Hollywood types, some Broadway people. And that right there is why I will *never* work with any of them. Such prima donnas."

"Who's the actor?" I pulled a repair kit out of the case to fix a string I broke during the soundcheck. I slipped the A-string through the pin on the bridge of my Martin.

"Fitz Baker. His new movie, *Fury*, opens on Friday. You know, it probably wouldn't be a bad idea to go down there. Try to make a good impression. You look so cute today with your hair all done."

"He sounds like a jerk." I frowned as I pulled the string up to the tuning peg. "Is he a big deal?"

"Um, if you consider an A-list actor and *People*'s Sexiest Man Alive a big deal. Didn't you ever watch *Bailey's Life*?"

I shook my head. "Nuh-uh. I never go to the movies."

"Well, that was a TV show. It was on for like ten years. And what about *City on the Hill*?"

Again, it was a no.

"Not even *The Dwelling*, the whole reason for tonight?" Callie was incredulous. "Come on, he's probably going to get an Oscar nom for it. It was amazing."

When I kept shaking my head, she scoffed.

"Cal, you know I've seen absolutely nothing. At home, all I ever watched was my mom's old collection, and for the last four years here, it's been music, school, work. Rinse and repeat." I tightened the string and plucked it, testing its pitch. Not quite. "Besides, who has money to blow on a fifteen-dollar movie ticket when rent is this bad? Clearly, the guy is a dick. I'll pass on his movies and on meeting him."

Calliope pulled out her phone.

"Here," she said after Googling his name. "That's him. Look familiar?"

He did, a little. I'd probably seen his face around in supermarket checkout lines or something like that. The Sexiest Man Alive cover was definitely a looker. He was every inch an American heartthrob: tall and tan, with muscles that were superhero-worthy without too much bulk. His smile was bright white under a tangle of golden hair and green eyes that were sharp as arrows. Lord. Yeah, I could definitely see why he won the title.

"Earth to Maggie. You still there?"

I shook my head and turned back to the guitar. "He looks very...punchable."

"I think you mean fuckable. But maybe both." Calliope took one last look at the photo before stowing her phone with a sigh. "I swear, if I ever did get the chance, I'd duct-tape his mouth shut. I can't believe he talks to his manager like that. Rumor has it he's got a drug problem bigger than the state of Rhode Island."

"Then I definitely don't want to meet him." I finished knotting the string and clipped the end before stowing my tools in the case. "Good as new."

Calliope watched as I finished tuning and strummed a few opening chords, humming along.

She smiled. "You're going to kill it, babe. Now, are you ready to do some serious networking? You can pass on the dickwad if you want, but there are a lot of others down there who need to know your name."

I looked over the balcony toward the stage. More and more people were filing in, along with a crowd of photographers and other members of the press. I doubted I'd actually appear in anything beyond my name as an opener, but it was extra publicity. Couldn't hurt.

I set my guitar in its case. "I'm ready as I'll ever be."

TWO HOURS LATER, the photocall was mostly over, although people were lingering around the stage, laughing, talking, and answering a few last-minute questions.

"Maggie Sharp," I said to the fourth interviewer. "I'm opening for Gillian tonight."

He looked me over appreciatively. "Score for you, huh? Did I hear your manager say you're an NYU student?"

I nodded, masking a frown. "I'm about to graduate. Just one more month."

That was the third time someone had asked me that. I was already being cast as Gillian's student charity case, and I wasn't a fan.

"Well, well. You planning to hang around after the show? I'd love to buy you a celebratory drink."

Fourth time for that particular offer. The reporter—who hadn't even offered a name—raised a suggestive brow. He was forty if he was a day.

I just smiled tightly. "Um, maybe. I'm sure I'll be around."

He grinned, then turned to talk to the manager of the venue, who was making a bunch of other people laugh. For what was probably the tenth time in the last two hours, I cast covertly around for the face from the magazine cover. I couldn't help it. He sounded like a dick, sure, but for some reason, I was curious. What made someone act like that? What made him hate this so much?

I'd caught the back of his head a few times, but he never turned, revealing only a broad set of shoulders in a thin gray T-shirt and a pair of jeans that hung over a sculpted backside and long legs.

He had done most of his part of the photocall and interviews before I was even allowed in front of the photographers and spent the rest of the time sulking around shadows and muttering to his manager. Then, about an hour ago, he'd disappeared.

But I couldn't seem to keep myself from looking again and again. It was just because the guy was famous, I told myself. Who wouldn't want to meet a celebrity, right? It had nothing to do with wanting to know if his eyes were as green as grass. Or the fact that even from the magazine cover, they seemed to see right through me.

Nothing at all.

"Smile."

I turned to Calliope, who was grinning across the way.

I frowned. "You look like the Cheshire cat. Why are you grinning like that?"

"That's Theo del Conte behind me staring at you," she said through her teeth. "His dad is Max de Conte, head of Del Conte Entertainment. The guy in the suit over there."

When I frowned some more, she huffed. "Girl, do you want a record deal or not? I'm your manager. Let me manage you! Now, paste a smile on that pretty face of yours and suck up to some corporates, all right?"

I snickered but turned obediently to look in the direction where she'd been smiling. A dark, somewhat foreboding man in a black suit was talking with Gillian. Several other people hovered around the periphery, including a younger, attractive man with shiny black hair and a matching goatee who was watching me with a friendly smirk.

I couldn't say why, but the whole party just gave me a bad feeling.

I turned back. "Cal. It's been two hours. I'm done."

"But—"

"I'm supposed to be on in about an hour, girl. These people are staying for the show, right?"

She nodded.

"Well, that's my best pitch. I'm going to get ready, okay?"

Calliope looked like she wanted to argue, but simply surveyed the rest of the crowded theater, allowing the population to speak for her. Now that the celebrities were gone, other people were starting to arrive. Important people. People I shouldn't avoid.

I didn't want to say it, but my stomach was a mess. Studio heads? Label CEOs? This gig was beyond a simple chance. It was a gift from God. And I was terrified I was going to blow it.

Callie turned to me, and immediately her irritation evaporated. Gone was the manager. My best friend was back.

"Go," she said kindly. "Get your head right. You're an incredible talent, Maggie, and I can't wait for the rest of the world to find out. You're going to kill it, and they'll be climbing over each other to get to you."

I smiled—this time genuinely. "Thanks, Cal."

With a quick hug that managed not to ruin my hair, I escaped back to the dressing room where I'd stowed the rest of my things. My instruments were already on the stage, but I had my old Yamaha in there to warm up my fingers. *I can do this*, I thought as I pushed open the door. Couldn't I?

"There's someone in here!"

The cry of a deep male voice made me jump.

"I—er—I, um—"

I was frozen at the door. Glancing around the room, there was no one there—until I noticed a shadow lurking behind the privacy screen in the corner. It was a man, obviously. A large man with big shoulders, hunched over in a seated position, hands gripping the back of his head. His entire posture screamed tension. And power.

My instinct was to back out like a scared kitten and let whatever grump was squatting here have it.

But then I remembered Callie's last words. I was an incredible talent. I was the incredible talent assigned to this dressing room. This was *my* sanctuary to find some calm before the show.

He needed to leave.

"I *said*, this room is occupied," snapped the voice, deep and insistent, with a scratch in the back of his throat.

That was it. I wasn't doing this anymore. I was tired of feeling scared and ignored and pushed around by people who thought they were so much more important than me. I was a performer. I needed space. That was all that mattered.

I checked the label on the door—which clearly bore my name—then turned back.

"Yes, it is occupied," I said. "By me."

SEVEN

Maggie

"This is my dressing room, sir," I tried again. "You're going to have to leave."

"I don't think so."

The man's voice cut like a machete. This time, however, I was impervious.

I scowled. "I'm not kidding. Get out."

"Look, miss. I—I just need a minute, okay? I'm k-kind of going through something. Would you mind?"

"Actually, I would mind," I snapped. "I'm Maggie Sharp, the opening act. That's my name on the door, not yours, whoever you are. And *I* need a minute in *my* dressing room!"

Did I sound like a diva? Maybe. But that's what rooms like this were for. I couldn't deal with some pretentious asshole stealing my space before the biggest break of my life.

"Look, I'll stay here behind the screen. You won't even know I'm here. I promise."

His voice had lost its imperiousness, though the slight

sharpness remained. His shoulders slumped, however, in defeat. He was begging, in his own way.

I frowned but let the door swing shut behind me. "What if I needed to get dressed?"

"Do you?"

I looked down at my blue dress, thinking of the hair I'd already primped and sprayed into place hours ago, the makeup that had been set to keep under the lights. "Well—no."

"Well, then." The voice relaxed a bit more, humor swimming below the bite.

Slowly, I moved to the dressing table next to the screen at the far end of the room and checked myself in the mirror. Everything seemed in order.

"Okay," I said. "It's been a minute. Look, I don't mean to be a jerk, but I go on in an hour, and I need to warm up. Prepare, you know?"

"I..." His voice sounded pained. Something about it twisted in a pitch at some inaudible frequency. It sounded like torture. "Please. Do you mind if I stay? I really don't really have anywhere to go, and I absolutely can't deal with all of that out there. I'll get out of your hair eventually, but I just need some time."

"Time for what?" I asked suspiciously. He didn't sound awful, but what if this guy was a drug addict or had some kind of fetish? I'd played in enough clubs to know that the types who usually had to sneak off were doing something they shouldn't. And I didn't have time to babysit a strung-out basket case right now.

"Just time," he replied. "Don't you ever need to just get away from people?"

I was about to ask him to leave again, but some other

latent note stopped me. I felt that need constantly. Like right now.

"Sometimes, yes. It's hard not to feel that way in this city," I admitted.

There was a sigh, long and low. "Yeah. I know."

"I live with three other girls in a two-bedroom apartment," I went on as I massaged my hand. "Two are artists, one's a sculptor, and there's me. We don't even have a TV. We have *no* space. Most of my half of the bedroom is taken up by guitars."

"Seriously?"

I rolled my eyes. Everyone thought it was crazy that a houseful of artists and musicians didn't watch TV. Well, it was a waste of time and money, in my mind. "Seriously."

The stranger snorted. "Well. You're not missing much."

"I figured."

Why was I even telling him all of this? This guy didn't know me. He was probably someone's assistant or maybe one of the security people. He didn't care about how some poor college student lived when she wasn't trying to strum her guitar.

I rubbed some lotion into my other hand, then started massaging the tendons too. The last thing I needed was my hand cramping up.

"I bet you want to be on TV, though," he said, his voice full of sudden bitterness. "Everyone wants to be famous."

"Not me."

The words came out before I could stop them, surprising me with their vehemence. Was that actually how I felt? Callie talked all the time about getting me on the *Tonight Show* or something like that one day. I never argued.

Now I stared at my polished fingernails, suddenly

unsure. I wasn't a natural on stage, but I also hadn't ever voiced that particular sentiment out loud.

The man snorted. "Sure. That's why you're performing tonight, right?"

I looked up. "Well, I'm not hiding away in a broom closet," I snapped, now defensive.

"Dressing room."

"Same difference." I waved around the tiny room, not caring that he probably couldn't see me.

But instead of responding with another quick retort, the stranger just laughed. And instead of making me angry, the sound actually relaxed my entire body, from my neck and shoulders down to the tips of my fingers. I exhaled.

"So, why are you here?" I asked as I turned to the mirror to check my makeup yet again. "Hiding away?" I tried to remember where I'd heard that voice before. It sounded kind of familiar, but I didn't think he was performing tonight. "You're not in one of the other bands, are you?"

A low, buttery chuckle floated through the screen. "God, no. I only wish I could be a rock star."

I couldn't help but laugh myself. His wry humor was kind of infectious. "So, what's the big deal out there for you?"

There was a long pause behind the screen, then the squeak of his chair as he shifted in his seat.

"My ex-girlfriend showed up at a, ah, meeting today," he said finally. "We used to work together. And she came, even though she wasn't supposed to. Now all the people I work with, well...they're here too, and they want to talk about it. But I don't." He sighed. "Gossip. It drives me fucking nuts."

"Me too," I agreed.

"Really?" He sounded honestly surprised.

"Well, yeah. It's bad for everyone. People like it because it makes them feel superior, but they never understand what it does to other people, being turned into objects of fascination."

He was quiet for a moment. "You sound like you know what that feels like."

I thought of my mom. Wondering what she was doing now. The salon was probably about to close, which meant she was finishing her last job. On a good day, she could go without a drink until five. The bad ones, she risked losing clients because she was cutting hair on vodka fumes. And then I'd learn about it at school the next day when their daughters would come to class after overhearing the chatter about Ellie Sharp and her latest drunken escapade.

"What did she do?" I changed the subject. "Your ex."

The stranger sighed. "Nothing awful. Not really. It was just manipulative. She came to support some other people who had a big event going on. But the whole time, she had to stand next to me. Smile at me. Be around me. It just reminded me and everyone else what it was like when we were together." He huffed. "I sound fucking pathetic, don't I?"

"No. You just sound sad. Did she—was it—was it a bad breakup?"

I wasn't sure if I should ask. But on the other hand, we *were* swapping stories.

"Yeah," he said quietly. "It was."

We sat together for a few more moments in silence while I touched up my eyeliner. It wasn't awkward. Actually, it was strangely easy. Peaceful.

"You're easy to talk to, Country."

"'Country'? Why 'Country'?"

"Don't you play country music? That's what we're here to listen to, right?"

I chuckled. "I guess so. Yeah, I play some country. More folk, I guess, but in the same bandwidth."

He chuckled too. The warm sound vibrated through the room, wrapping around me like a hug. "Maybe it's the screen. Maybe it's just easier to talk to someone you can't actually see. Like confession, but without the guilt."

"Can't you just tell them to mind their own business?" I wondered, still thinking about the story he'd told me. "And ask your ex to leave?"

He snorted again. "I fucking wish. This isn't the first time she's done it, and everyone loves her. People are nosy, you know? They find out a few things about you, and they just think they know everything. Suddenly, that's all you are."

"Oh." My heart felt for the guy. The utter despondency in his voice. "Yes, I know how that is."

"Oh, yeah? How's that?"

I turned to where my Yamaha stood on a stand and traced the edge of my finger along the guitar's veneer edge. This wasn't something I liked to talk about. At least, not outside of my music.

But the stranger was right. Maybe it was easier to be open without someone looking at you.

"My mother's an alcoholic," I said as I picked up the guitar and set it on my knee to warm up. "And a—well, she gets around."

"So does everyone in this business. Why is it a bad thing if your mom likes to have fun?"

"Spoken like a man," I said wryly.

To my surprise, he laughed. Most men would get defensive, but he seemed to see the irony in his statement.

"Touché," he said. "But beyond a bad reputation..."

"It was a bad thing when she was too blitzed to remember to pay the electricity bills," I said as I worked through a scale. "And it was bad when her 'friends' would come exploring her little girl's bedroom."

"They didn't—with you—" His voice was thick, tripping like he was wearing shoes two sizes too big.

"No," I quickly supplied. "Not that. After the first one came prowling around, I moved to a guest cabin on our property, along with a couple of padlocks. They never knew I was there after that. But I was only twelve, you know."

There was another long silence, which I filled with a D scale on my guitar. My fingers were warming now. No need to massage the tension out.

"Do you ever go back?"

I shook my head, even though he couldn't really see me. Or maybe he could, I thought as I squinted at the screen. It wasn't totally opaque. This close through the rose-colored silk, I could make out the silhouette of a floppy head of hair, a man's square jaw and straight nose, and the outline of a pair of full lips. I had the lights behind me—he could probably see my entire silhouette perfectly.

"I haven't been back in two years," I told him while picking out a simple Travis pattern. "The last time I visited, she sold my Gibson to pay her phone bill."

The guitar wasn't even the worst of it, though I didn't say so. The worst was when she slapped me across the face four separate times after I continued to demand she pay me back. The worst was when I told her in two years it would be me or the bottle and she told me not to come back the next summer.

So I didn't.

"What about your family?" I asked. "Are you better than what you came from?"

The stranger seemed to think for a long time, long enough that I was able to get through three more scales.

"Maybe," he said finally. "It's hard to say. My parents are, well, they hate each other, to start. And they don't like me much either. I haven't lived with either one for a long time. We don't get along."

"Why do they hate you?" I asked. "You don't seem so bad."

There was a low laugh. "I can be difficult, I guess."

I considered the number of times my mother had said just that to me.

Maggie Mae, stop being so difficult.

Why do you always have to make things so hard, Margaret?

It was usually when I was saying things she didn't want to hear. Things like, *That's enough for tonight, Mama,* or *Please don't bring that man back to the house, Mama.*

"Me too," I said.

"So you left because you wanted to be someone else?"

"No," I said. "I left because I didn't want to be her bastard kid anymore or anything like her at all. I wanted to be something else besides...that." I sighed. "So now I've got this hipster Loretta Lynn thing going on, but that's not really me either."

"Hipster Loretta Lynn? I'm having a hard time imagining that."

The stranger chuckled again, and this time his deep voice vibrated down to the pit of my belly, where it loosened the ball of nerves lodged there.

"Blue ruffles. Big hair. But, you know, very tasteful," I

joked. "You want to see?" I set my guitar back on the stand and made to rise, but his voice stopped me.

"No, no, I'm good," he said. "I can't spoil the surprise now, can I?"

He laughed some more, and I slumped, relishing in the comfort of the sound. I didn't even know this man, but somehow, just his presence relaxed me.

"Seriously, though," he said. "If you don't like it, why do it? Why not just look yourself? Seems like a perk of the music industry. You get to be you."

I stared at myself in the mirror. I looked good. I looked very attention-getting. The dress was very blue and very short. My hair framed my face in far more manicured waves than I ever had time for. Callie had spent a full forty-five minutes on my makeup, plus a touch-up before the photocall.

"Sometimes people can't listen if they don't like what they see," I said. "I just want them to hear me. *Me.*" I shook my head. I didn't think I'd ever said any of that out loud before either. "I just don't know if they can do it. If *I* can do it."

"You sound scared."

I sucked in a deep breath. "I am."

EIGHT

Will

I just wanted to keep her talking. I probably should have left the second she came in, but I couldn't remember the last time I'd spoken to someone like this, if ever. Frank and open, without that jittery expression fans got or the calculated look of reporters and industry execs. Like I was just a person, not a name, a face, a thing.

But this girl—Maggie—had no idea she was talking to someone the whole world thought they knew. To her, I was just an eccentric stranger behind a flimsy piece of cloth. It was the first honest conversation I'd had in years. Maybe my entire life.

When she invited me to take a look at her dress, I almost stood up. Honestly, part of me wanted to see what she would do once I showed my face. Would she keep talking? Act like nothing had changed? Maybe we could talk some more. Maybe I'd ask her to meet me after the show so we could do it some more.

But she'd know, a voice whispered in the back of my

mind. And once people realized who I was, they stopped doing this. They stopped treating me like me.

"What about you?" she was saying. "Do you live with a lot of people?"

I smirked. "No."

What would she say if I told her about the compound in Vermont? Or the Central Park penthouse I was considering?

"Sometimes I feel like I share a room with everyone in the world, though." It was as close as I'd ever get to telling her the truth.

Then she surprised me again.

"That sounds lonely, actually."

I stilled. Maybe she knew after all. How else could she understand what I meant by that?

"How do you figure?" Suspicion spiked my words like cheap vodka.

"Well, if everyone is in the room together, there's no privacy just to get to know one person. And would you know if they were *really* being themselves? You couldn't. Not with everyone watching. You'd all be together, but at the same time, you'd never *really* be together. Does that make sense?"

I stared at the screen, mouth open. It made complete sense. *Too* much sense. How was it possible that someone who had never even seen my face could describe everything wrong with my life in a few short sentences?

A roar of noise gushed through the closed dressing room door as the crowd yowled. Jake Fletcher, a comedian and one of the supporting actors from *Fury*, had agreed to do a short set before the music started. That and the fact that the headliner had recorded the film's soundtrack joined the two groups together and kicked off the whole *Fury* press tour.

Through the screen, the bright lights of the dressing room mirror cast the girl's body in a clear silhouette. So I could tell she had long hair piled over one graceful shoulder, hunched slightly with anxiety. Sometimes, when she turned in profile, I could make out a small, straight nose and a pair of lips a lot of women paid big money for. Once, I even saw a shadow of eyelashes as they swept closed. It was hard not to stare when that happened. But I did anyway, because shit, she couldn't see me. I told myself they were fake. No one was naturally that beautiful just in silhouette.

She rubbed her hands together, then pressed them to her face. "You can do this," she whispered.

I wondered if she meant for me to hear it.

"Are you all right?" I asked.

She started on her chair, as if only just realizing I was still here.

"Oh, um, yeah. Nerves. I was only offered this gig a couple of weeks ago, and I've never done anything like it. Usually I just play local bars, coffee shops. Places like that."

I let out a long whistle. "Nice work. How did you get it?" Please don't say you slept with the booker.

For some reason, the idea made me want to break something.

"Through my manager, Calliope Jackson. She's—well, it's sort of a fluke, honestly. She's my best friend—we're both at NYU together. But she's been interning for this firm for the last two years and found out that Gillian lost her opener. So she submitted my tape and made it happen. I'm her first real client, and this is my first real gig."

She giggled nervously, and hell if the sound didn't echo through my bones. I felt warmer. Lighter. I wanted to make her do it some more.

College. Okay. So she was really young. Brand new to

all of this. That meant the lips, the eyelashes, all of it was the genuine article. Struggling musicians couldn't pay for things like injections and extensions.

"So this is your..." I trailed off.

"This is my shot," she said softly.

I could have done the nice thing and reassured her with words like "Don't worry yourself" or "There are other shots if you mess up." But the hard truth was, there generally aren't. She knew it. I knew it. Everyone in this building would know it too the second this girl stumbled under the bright stage lights with eyes like Bambi.

I thought back to the photocall, trying to remember who all showed up. Three other bands besides Maggie, right? Gillian and the second headliner were both big enough that they didn't give a shit who I was. The third was a smaller jug band, but they had a manager, an agent, and a bunch of T-shirts they were selling at the merch table.

And then there was Maggie Sharp. Where had she been? Did the *Rolling Stone* reporters care enough to interview her? Had she stood in front of the photographers by the stage? I had been on the tail end of my afternoon high. I couldn't remember half the faces I met, half the hands I shook. Somewhere in all that commotion had been this girl. Maggie. And I missed her.

Fuck.

"What if they realize I'm a fraud?" she said, her voice shaking slightly. "I came to New York to make my mark."

"Where from?" I asked, trying to distract her. I would have bet my bank account she wasn't from the East Coast. There was too much lilt in her speech. She didn't move fast enough, like most uptight New Englanders.

"Eastern Washington. This tiny community right on the border of Idaho." She took a deep breath and sighed. "All my life, my talent was the only thing I'd been able to claim as my own. But what if the truth is, I'm just not good enough?"

I was silent, feeling her nerves right along with her. I wanted to ask why she felt she wasn't good enough and for who, but found I already understood. I wouldn't know until I heard her, but this girl obviously wasn't a natural performer. Natural performers don't hide out in dressing rooms hours before they go on. They don't talk to strangers about their life's problems instead of posing for photographers. They live for the attention, stare at their reflections at the end of a camera lens, ready to drown in the heady sheen of their warped self-portraits, like Narcissus.

That wasn't this girl any more than it was me. And you know, I liked her all the more for it.

Her breathing grew jagged on the other side of the screen, and her shoulders vibrated with each exhale. And for just a moment, I forgot about the mountain of shit waiting for me on the other side of those doors. Amy. Benny. Mom. Dad. A thousand voices, a thousand questions.

For one second, this tiny room held everything that mattered. This girl was scared. And I would have given everything I had to make her feel better.

"Here."

I reached around the screen before I could stop myself. She turned, stiffening with surprise, her chin tucked adorably as she looked down at my hand.

"It's big," she observed.

"That's what she said." I winced. "Sorry. That was terrible."

For a moment, I thought she might kick me out. It was a gross joke, but the type I heard almost daily in the world I lived in. Most men in the industry couldn't have cared less about offending a girl like Maggie. If anything, they would try just to see how far across the line she'd let them go.

Fuck. I didn't want to be that guy. Especially not now. Not with her.

To my utter relief, there was only another giggle at my self-chastisement, a soft, winsome sound that made me feel like I was floating about three inches off my chair. That is, until she set her hand in mine, and I honestly thought I might hit the ceiling.

This was better than any high. This simple touch.

Her fingers were long and slender, weaving between mine automatically as if they belonged there. Absently, I ran my thumb over her knuckles and the smooth skin covering her delicate bones, the contours of her wrist. Her nails were smooth under my fingers, curved but not too long, and she wore no jewelry. Not a ring or a bracelet. Just her skin and that soft pulse under my fingertips.

"Your hand is warm." She sighed, clearly content. "Too bad you can't hold mine through my whole set."

"Too bad," I agreed, more to myself than to her.

For a second, I imagined it and more. Walking the red carpet with this hand in mine. Holding her tight through a sea of questions and people. Guiding her through the mobs but focusing on this slight touch like a wayfinder in the dark. For the first time in a long time, it actually seemed doable.

This hand, small as it was, made me feel like I could do anything.

Or maybe it was just that no one else had held mine in so long, I'd forgotten what it was like not to have to do this shit alone.

"How do they do it?" Maggie wondered. "How do these

people get up in front of everyone night after night and not get sick?"

"Some do," I replied. "Stage fright is no joke."

"There's got to be some way to make it better. I feel like I really am going to throw up."

"Well, the only thing I know that helps is getting high or getting laid." It was only after the words came out that I realized what a huge dick I sounded like.

"What?"

And now I was back to thrilled she couldn't see me, because I was bright fucking red. Jesus *Christ*. Did I really just suggest that this girl fuck away her nerves? Who is she? Me?

"Does that actually work?"

"Ah, which one? Drugs or sex?"

She paused for a second. "Both. Drugs. No, sex. I don't like drugs."

"Yeah, no. Me neither."

Total fucking lie.

I could practically hear her brain working, figuring out how each of the two options would work legitimately. Of course, she wasn't one for drugs. Not given what she'd said about her mother. Sex, though...

I found myself folding my hand tightly around hers, despite the fact that she hadn't tried to pull away at all. I was pretty sure she could feel my palm getting sweaty, but I wasn't sure I cared.

"Ahh, yeah," I admitted. "I mean, I won't lie. Sex helps. Sometimes."

Her fingers curled into my palm. "Are you on stage a lot?"

"I, um, do a good amount of public speaking."

Tell her. I should have. But I didn't. Because I was a selfish bastard, and I was enjoying this too much.

Maggie giggled. It was fucking adorable.

"Next thing I know, you're going to suggest helping me out," she said.

I stiffened, both in my chair and, yeah, under my jeans. I couldn't help it. Just the idea of coming around that screen made me half-hard. I didn't need to see her face to know she was beautiful. Even her shadow had curves. And now she was actually suggesting it? Fuck.

"I mean, if you want me to…" I stumbled over the words. Which I usually didn't. Ever.

She laughed again. This time full-out laughed. And maybe I was still dealing with a high, but it sounded like a damn babbling brook right out of a Disney movie, where I was a stupid rabbit or a fox or whatever that's completely twitterpated? That's the word, right? Twitterpated.

Or maybe it really was just the last of the Percocet and whatever Benny gave me that was making my heart thump like this. Whatever it was, I didn't care. And I wasn't letting go of this hand for anything.

"I'm good," she said, still chuckling here and there. "Thanks for offering, though."

I wanted her to laugh some more. "You sure, beautiful? If you want, I could do it for you. Make you forget your own name, along with the crowd out there, if you know what I mean."

At that, the hand in mine finally jerked. "*What?*"

I grinned. I really was an asshole, but now I couldn't help myself from pressing on. Her hand was still here. Which told me she was at least a little interested in where this was going.

"Are you the kind of girl who would let a stranger you met two minutes ago screw you in your dressing room, Maggie? Because if you are, just say the word. I'd be happy to oblige."

There was a long silence. The laughter was gone. Now the air in the little room crackled, but with what, I wasn't sure. Shock? Irritation? Maybe curiosity?

"No."

And then, to my dismay, Maggie pulled her hand out of my grasp, leaving my palm empty and cold. She shifted in her seat, and for a moment, I thought she might leave.

Until she sighed. And didn't move.

"You want to know something, Maggie Sharp?" I asked.

"What?" She sounded more than a little pissed off.

"I'm glad," I said softly.

I kept my hand where it was and flexed it open. Her head moved behind the screen, turned down. She was looking at my fingers, considering. I watched her hand rise from her knee, and a few seconds later, she set it back in my palm. Caution sang through her touch. Caution and maybe desire.

I squeezed. "I'm glad," I told her again. "You don't seem the type."

"Would—would you *really* do something like that? Screw someone you didn't know, and then just leave them to calm yourself down?" Her voice was timid but obviously curious.

For a moment, I considered lying. I considered telling her that I was the type of guy who only made love on warm summer nights, just like one of her country songs. Spin her a story about how I'd only had a few other women I'd loved and lost, and now I needed a girl like her to help me sew the pieces of my broken heart back together.

She probably would have eaten it right up. They always did.

But I knew I could never be anything but honest with this girl. Maggie Sharp. Whoever she was.

"If you'd asked me that an hour ago, the answer was probably yes," I said truthfully. She would think I was a grade A shit, but at least it was the real me. "But with you? No. Because now I know you."

There was another long pause. She was disgusted with me, I knew it. I prepared myself to get kicked out, probably sold out to the tabloids for sexually harassing a singer.

But she surprised me. Instead of telling me to leave like we both knew she should, Maggie said the absolute last thing I expected: "What...what would you do instead?"

NINE

Maggie

Oh. My. God.

I couldn't believe I had just asked him that.

But even then, I didn't walk it back. I didn't apologize or laugh or anything. Because for the first time that night, my stomach didn't feel like it was about to empty itself.

At first, his boldness was off-putting. He had been trying to shock me, test me a little to see what I'd do. I didn't like being manipulated any more than I liked being ignored. But when I'd called his bluff, those big shoulders had relaxed again, and he'd grabbed at his hair in a gesture so endearingly dejected that I almost tore the screen down to give him a hug.

Now, though, I just wanted an answer to my question.

What would *he* do to me now that he knew I "wasn't the type?"

"Maggie, I—"

"Just tell me," I interrupted. "You don't get to screw me, but I wouldn't mind a distraction. Plus, you just embarrassed me, so now it's my turn. Do it, smart-ass. How does it start?"

In my mind, he was tall, dark, and handsome. With just the right amount of scruff and a body like Captain America, with the willingness to dart around the screen, pin my wrists behind my back, and make me forget my nerves. I knew that, in reality, the thumb that had started stroking over my knuckles probably belonged to a middle-aged man with a beer belly, shadows be damned.

But for now, the fantasy was doing it for me. And I would have taken *anything* to keep this blissful calm going.

"That depends," he said, like he was finding it hard to speak clearly. "On, well, on what you like. What you sound like. What happens when we kiss. Do you—" He cleared his throat roughly. "Do you like being kissed, Maggie?"

Did I like to be kissed?

His chair leg squeaked on the floor as he shifted in his seat. He turned directly toward me, making his shoulders look even wider than before, tapering down to a waist that couldn't be confused with any kind of belly. I caught a silhouette of hair—a mop of something messy that he liked to push his hand through.

"Who doesn't?" I asked, inwardly cursing my unnecessarily breathy voice. "Everyone likes being kissed. A good kiss is, well, a good kiss makes you forget everything."

I closed my eyes, trying to remember the last time someone had ever made me feel that way. My first kiss had been with my first boyfriend, Lucas, sitting at the end of his dock while the sun set over the lake back home. It was nice, but it hadn't made me feel much more than that. Nor had it for the two years we dated before I left for New York.

If it had been that great, I probably wouldn't have left. Right?

Still, I'd had a few short relationships in college and enjoyed a few wild nights after a gig or open mic. I knew what it felt like to be kissed until my heart picked up a few beats. Or how it could feel when a man—a *real* man—sucked on my lips like candy and grabbed my ass in *just* the right way. I was young, but I wasn't that young.

"I'd probably like kissing you," the stranger admitted.

I licked my lips and watched as his blurry shape moved again, like he couldn't get comfortable. I could definitely understand that. A kiss that made me forget? I had thought I knew what that was like, but right now, I wondered if I knew anything at all.

"Then what?" I asked though I was almost scared to hear the answer.

"Then I'd..." he drifted off, like he was unsure of what to say. "Are you sure you want me to talk about this?" The broad hand holding mine squeezed. "I kind of like just doing this, you know. It calms me down, too."

I gulped. "I—look, if you don't, I'll probably start having an anxiety attack and ruin the whole show. You said this would be distracting. So far it is. So, yeah. Keep going."

I found myself wondering what the stranger's experience was. I bet that deliciously low voice was *great* at whispering sweet—or sultry—nothings into a woman's ear. I wondered how many times he had done it before.

That thought made me want to throw my hairbrush into the mirror. Whoa.

"Okay," he said, pulling me out of my irrationally jealous thoughts. "Well, I'd kiss you. A lot. Use my tongue if you like. I'd want to learn what you taste like, Maggie. As much as you let me. Until you run out of breath and can barely moan, much less speak."

I swallowed thickly. "I—okay."

"Then I'd run my hands down your neck," he continued, apparently needing no more encouragement. "Over your shoulders and arms. Up your back and around your waist. Just a little at first, to get the feel of your body. And if you whimpered or moaned or anything, I'd probably drift my fingers up your ribcage. Maybe tickle the undersides of your breasts. See how far you'd let me go. See if maybe they'd fit in my palms."

My breath hitched. I couldn't help it. I stared down at the hand wrapped around mine, already imagining it over my breast. He had large, tan palms and strong fingers that were currently stroking circles at the base of my thumb. They seemed deft and capable. Good at pinching, maybe. Pulling.

I gulped. Good lord.

"You're, um, quite the lover, aren't you?" I asked, struggling to find my voice again.

"Hard to say. But I think I could get there with you, Maggie."

He was teasing, but maybe not. Judging by the electric current racing between our hands at the moment, this guy was a regular Don Juan. I bet he would know *exactly* how to make me moan in any way he wanted.

His fingernail scratched the center of my palm. It was everything I could do not to knock the screen over.

"And then what?" I asked, my voice barely audible above the hum of the crowd outside. Would I even be able to sing after this? I wasn't sure I cared.

"And then..."

I closed my eyes, letting my other hand rest idly on my bare knee, slipping under my skirt and drifting over my skin. Like maybe his would. I wondered if he was doing the same thing. Maybe it would make us both complete perverts, but

I wondered if he was touching himself at all on the other side of the screen. Maybe his hand was resting over a very *nice* bulge in his jeans. Feeling desire throb, dying for my touch as much as I was currently dying for his.

"You said you're wearing a dress?" he asked, deep voice slightly strained.

I didn't speak—I couldn't, just recrossed my legs and nodded. Luckily, he chuckled and continued.

"Well, I'd probably cop a feel, then." The hand holding mine squeezed. "Like that, only instead of your hand, it would be your ass. And if you liked it, I'd probably slip my hand further down, right between those beautiful legs, and..."

My mouth dropped, and I sat back stiffly, trying to ignore the throbbing between my legs. It had been a long time.

"I bet you'd be wet," he said softly. "But I wouldn't take you. Not—not yet."

I snorted. "Most would."

"I'd like to think I'm not most men."

There was another soft chuckle, but when I didn't respond, he kept going, to my delight.

"I'd find your clit first," he said. "With my other hand. See what happens when I touch it. Stroke it. Maybe pinch it. Fuck you with my other hand until you completely. Fall. Apart."

I leaned closer to the screen so I was maybe a foot away from him.

"It all depends on what *you* like, beautiful."

My other hand rose to my chest, just over my heart, which was full-on racing by that point. Lord, I could barely breathe. I hoped he was having just as hard a time.

"You sound like a v-very generous lover," I said, cursing

that stupid stutter. I was trying to mock him, but the catch undercut the joke.

He just laughed softly again, a low, smooth rumble through the room. "And all the while, I'd never stop."

"Stop—stop what?" My voice was barely audible.

"Kissing you."

"This is crazy," I whispered. "I can't believe we're even talking about this."

"You want me to keep going? We haven't even gotten to the good part yet."

I half wanted to say yes. To beg him to tell me all the different ways he'd defile my body. On the floor. The couch. The dressing table. How he'd rip this pretty stage dress and make us both forget exactly where we were and *who* we were for at least fifteen minutes.

Whoever he was in the first place.

"Would you really have t-taken me?" I wondered with my eyes closed. "Right here, if I had said yes?"

But he didn't answer right away. His breathing had turned heavy too, like he was struggling to catch up in a run. "I, well, it's like I said. An hour ago, I might have. But the truth is, the more I sit here with you, the more I don't want to be that guy anymore."

I was quiet for a long time. One *hour* ago? Who was this person? I sighed, rubbing a hand over my face but careful not to disturb Calliope's carefully drawn makeup.

"Then what do you want?" I wondered.

You. I wanted him to say it so badly. Even if we barely knew each other. Even if he came in here for something else an hour ago.

"Not that," he said, settling for a half answer. "Something better. Would you...Maggie, would you let me try something?"

I frowned at the hand clasped over mine. His fingers had tensed, and his grip tightened only slightly, like he was afraid I might flee.

"What's that?" I asked. I was still smarting a bit from the fact that he apparently didn't want to sleep with me. I didn't know why it mattered so much that a stranger I'd never actually seen didn't want me. But it did. Somehow, it mattered a lot. Too much.

"How about a hug?"

I raised a brow. "A hug?" It sounded woefully childlike. I wasn't going to admit it, but at this point, sight unseen, I wanted a lot more than a hug.

"I just want to touch you. Is that wrong?"

Oh. Well.

"I don't think so." I smiled. "But kind of hard to hug me if you don't want us to look at each other, don't you think?"

I could practically feel his grin through the silk.

"Maybe. But I like a challenge. Would you keep your eyes closed? For the sake of the distraction, I mean."

"I suppose it is like a kind of meditation," I joked.

It was absurd, this little game we were playing. We weren't fooling anyone, much less ourselves. Hugging someone you couldn't see was not normal. And I never did things like this. Flirting with a stranger in the back of a bar—that was my mother's play, not mine.

And yet here I was, playing his game. And only too happy to do so, considering it was the only thing, so far, distracting me from my nerves. Desire was burning away the butterflies in my belly. Anticipation is a powerful thing.

"All right," I said. "I'll keep my eyes closed. But you have to do the same."

"Me? I thought you didn't care if I saw you."

"Fair's fair," I countered. "I don't like an uneven advantage."

There was a low chuckle, the kind I could imagine with a smile full of promise and love.

Love? God, what was I on tonight.

But the stranger's touch was kind and warm. It left no room for me to doubt myself. Not now.

"All right," he said. "Stand up. But don't let go of my hand."

"Never," I joked. "Not even when I go onstage."

Again, there was that hint of laughter. I wanted more. I wanted to swim in that rumble and wrap myself in its warmth like a blanket on a cold night.

I closed my eyes and carefully pushed myself off my chair so I was standing. True to his word, the stranger did not release my hand or open his eyes—or so I assumed from the sound of his feet stumbling on the concrete floor. Another hand wrapped around my other wrist, and I stumbled too as I was pulled a few steps forward until my nose smacked into a broad chest. I turned my head to lay my cheek against his shirt, thrilling a bit. He was tall–much taller than me. Just as warm as he sounded. And no belly that I could sense.

The hands at my wrists fell away, then traveled up my arms, pausing every so often as if to take note of each contour. They were large and warm, like the rest of him, slightly calloused but capable as they slid over my shoulders. One reversed course, moved back down my arm, then slid around my waist where it pulled me closer until our bodies were completely flush. The other slipped around my neck to cup the back of my head, coaxing me to lie against his chest.

His body was warm—warmer than mine—and before I

realized it, my own hands had crept to his hips, slipping around his waist and up his back with the enjoyment of simple exploration. He was quite a bit taller than me, based on the fact that my chin nested comfortably in the hollow about his collarbone, and I was wearing boots with two-inch heels. His body, though, was trim and solid, the muscles of his waist and back alternately flexing and relaxing under my fingertips.

At his hips, I detected a waistband of frayed denim, a cracked leather belt that had almost certainly seen better days, and the edge of an impossibly soft T-shirt that smelled mildly of men's cologne, soap, and nicotine. Nothing fancy, then, unlike the majority of the people who had shown up here tonight. Most of the pseudo-celebrities and artists were either in designer duds or stage wear. He was probably a stagehand or a roadie, then. Maybe temporary waitstaff. Definitely not a part of the pomp and circumstance that had taken over the evening.

The thought soothed.

"You need to quit smoking," I mumbled.

"I need to quit a lot of things."

I didn't ask what. Right now, I didn't really want to know.

We stayed like that for several minutes, long past the point where I should have become uncomfortable. I didn't though. I could have stayed there forever.

"I knew it," he murmured into my hair.

"Knew what?" My voice was breathy, almost unintelligible, against his chest.

"That you were beautiful."

I snorted. "You have no idea what I look like."

The hand at my waist squeezed lightly. "I know enough."

I considered arguing but found I didn't want to.

We stood there for a moment, the gap between us completely closed as he cocooned me against his body. I felt my heart rate drop into a strong, steady thump, like it was prepared for action, but completely relaxed, too.

He was right. This was exactly what I needed.

"Maggie?"

"Mmm."

"I changed my mind."

I burrowed deeper on instinct. "About what?"

"About wanting more."

The hand at my waist slid to the small of my back and started stroking through the thin fabric of my dress. A shudder of tension rippled through me but in a good way.

"Oh—oh?"

Both of his hands traveled back to my shoulders, then up my neck, finally cupping my jaw to coax my face upward. Like I was looking, though my eyes were still shut. Oddly, I felt like I could see more clearly than ever.

"Can I kiss you?"

His breath was warm as it whispered over my lips. I wondered for a moment if he had cheated and opened his eyes, but I decided he hadn't. Not by the way the pads of his fingers were still drifting over my skin, exploring. Not by the way his thumbs were playing over my bottom lip, as if to memorize every plump curve.

On instinct, I pressed up on my tiptoes and touched my nose to his. "All right."

Slowly, his mouth found mine. His lips were full and soft but still firm, tentative at first until he seemed to learn the terrain. After that, he took control, slipping his tongue in to locate mine, twisting, turning them together in a delicate step I'd never danced before.

I opened to his touch like a flower. He tasted good. Familiar but intoxicatingly new. As one of his arms wrapped firmly around my shoulder, pulling me even closer, my own arms rose to pull him down and intensify the kiss.

On and on we went. Minutes, maybe. Perhaps hours. I honestly couldn't tell. All the time, I kept my eyes firmly shut. I could have opened them. He probably would have to. But we'd made a promise, and there was something about that promise that felt sacred. For whatever reason, I had the idea that my stranger wasn't given to trusting many people. His trust in me felt like a gift. I was determined to prove worthy.

At last, I broke away with a gasp, desperate for breath. I expected him to continue the kiss, but instead, I felt the touch of his forehead to mine.

"Thanks," he whispered.

"You're welcome." It was all I could manage.

We stood like that a minute more. My thighs were aching, and my breasts were swollen. I wanted more. I wanted him to do what he had originally suggested, shove me atop the dressing room counter and do what he wanted with me any way he liked.

Suffice it to say, I wanted a lot more than a kiss. And I found myself believing he wouldn't judge me for it. Not one bit.

"What are you thinking?" my stranger wondered.

I opened my mouth to tell him. But before I could reply, there was a knock at the door. He dropped my hand just as the squeaky hinges opened. I jumped and swung toward the door just as it opened.

"Maggie?" George's voice was older, calloused around the edges as he looked curiously around the dressing room.

"We're 'bout ready to start, hon, if you want to meet me and the boys out there."

I nodded as all the nerves in my stomach returned. *Here we go.* "Be right there, George."

The door closed, and I turned back to where my stranger was standing. He had used my distraction, however, to duck back behind the screen.

"I—everything okay?" I asked.

"Don't worry about me," said the stranger. "Get yourself ready to go. Relaxed now?"

I felt myself redden. "Ah, yes. Um, thank you."

A glance in the mirror told me I looked anything but relaxed. My cheeks were a little flushed, my hair was slightly mussed, and my skirt was twisted out of place. Carefully, I did my best to get myself back in order, though the motions only recalled the nerves all over again. Holy crap. This was it. In a few minutes, I had my one chance to make it. Or not.

And instead of preparing, I'd been making out with a complete and total stranger, sight unseen.

What was wrong with me?

"You're going to be great, Maggie." His deep voice shook me out of my thoughts from behind the screen.

"I—thank you," I said, staring at the reflection of the pink silk screen in the mirror. "And thank you for, you know."

My cheeks pinked even more.

"It was my pleasure. Will you play something for me before you go?"

I stared at my guitar, laying in its open case. Originally, I had come in here to warm up, but I had done enough of that before the photocall. My throat was ready. My fingers were ready. But was *I*?

The clock over the door said there was no time.

"I'd like to. But I have to go."

"Okay," the stranger said. "Hey, break a leg, all right? You'll do great. I'll be out there, rooting for you."

I turned back to the screen. "Please," I asked. "Can't I just see you?"

He didn't answer for a long time. The seconds ticked by, one by one, as I tried to wait him out. The truth was, I was dying to tear down that flimsy piece of silk between us. It was strange to bare your soul in the ways we just had and not even want to look a person in the face. But I didn't have forever. I had a show to get to, and this man, this strange, secretive man, couldn't take up all my time, much as I might want to let him.

His answer was still a blow.

"No."

My jaw dropped. "Are you serious?"

"How about this?" he hurried on. "I don't want to mess up your state of mind here, so instead, I'll come find you after the show, all right? I won't miss a thing. You can pretend I'm next to you if you need. Holding your hand."

I stood there a moment longer, considering. "I could just look. I could just come around the screen and look. You have nowhere to run."

Somehow, I sensed that we faced each other, the rose-colored silk fluttering slightly between us. My heart rate seemed to double at the idea of tearing it down—whether from desire or fear, I couldn't tell.

"I know," he said softly. "But you won't, will you?"

I emitted a long, low sigh. "Not if you don't want me to."

He reached out a hand, and I watched transfixed as it pressed through the silk, its outline dark as the thin fabric plastered over long, sturdy fingers and wide palm. Then he pulled it back, and my shoes clipped over the concrete floor as I grabbed my guitar, slung it around my shoulders, and moved to the door.

"I tell you what," I said. "I have a song called 'The Lonely.' When I play it tonight, I'll look for you. Where will you be sitting?"

There was another pause. "On the top floor. Wherever the VIP section is."

VIP? A stagehand or server wouldn't be in the VIP section. Who was this guy?

"Well, all right then," I said. "When I play it, I'll look up there. And you'll know that song's for you."

I opened the door, and immediately the buzz of the crowd filtered in from beyond the stage. Every muscle I had tightened, and I squeezed my eyes shut. Somehow, I had to walk onto that stage and command it. And I would do it. Because my stranger would be watching. Whoever he was.

A thought occurred.

No. It couldn't be.

"You're not that actor, are you?" I wondered, calling over the sound of the crowd. "Fitz something?"

There was a light rattle from behind the screen and the screech of a chair leg on the cement floor, like the question had startled him.

Immediately, I felt like a fool. Of course he wasn't that toxic actor. My stranger was kind and empathetic, not the toxic narcissist I'd overheard earlier. That guy was probably out in the crowd hitting on women and finding whatever his next high was going to be. A celebrity wasn't the kind of person who needed to recover from anxiety in the back of a dressing room.

"No," confirmed the stranger with the warm, large hands. "No, I've never been Fitz Baker."

Relief flooded through me. "Okay, good."

"Thank you for keeping me company, Maggie. Will I..." Something like doubt laced his voice. "Where will you be? After the show?"

I perked. "Back here?"

I wondered if he was smiling. Suddenly, I couldn't stop my own silly grin.

"Yeah. Right back here."

I nodded as the crowd sounded even louder. "It's a date. But if you're not Fitz, what *is* your name? I feel like I should at least know that."

"Maggie! Come on, hon!" a voice shouted from the hall.

"I'm sorry. I—I have to go," I said. "I'll see you after the show, whoever you are!"

"Sure," he called. "And my name is—"

The door swung shut before I could make out the last word. Well, I'd learn it later, anyway. And with a huge smile still plastered on my face, I walked down the hall toward the stage that would mark the beginning or the end of my music career.

TEN

Will

"I changed my mind."

I plopped down next to Benny after one of the stagehands escorted me through the staff corridors to the VIP section on the second floor. It wouldn't have been necessary, except the first time I tried to make my way out of that stupid maze, I ended up in the kitchen with six waitresses looking at me like I was a meal they wanted to eat, not serve.

Benny looked up from the two girls sitting on either side of him, then tossed his head, indicating that they needed to get up. One girl gave him a sorry look while the other examined me like she was also at the meat market. I just glared.

Benny grabbed his drink from the table and held it up. "You want one?"

I shook my head, and at that, he finally looked surprised. "Please don't tell me you took the rest of that Percocet in your pocket, man. I can't have you leaving the club on a stretcher, you got me? Too many studio heads and PR people here."

I clamped a hand on my jacket pocket, only to find it empty. And while the idea might have given me the shakes even hours ago, right now, I felt completely clear-headed.

"No," I said. "Fuck that shit. I'm done with it."

Benny just gave me a look. "Ohhhkay. What do you mean, you changed your mind?"

"About co-promoting with the musicians for the film. I think it's a good idea after all." I kept my gaze focused on him, ignoring the eager looks around us as more and more people realized I'd entered the VIP section. Fucking vultures. But right now, I couldn't care less. "Think about it. The artists are all touring together, right?"

Benny reared. "You know about that?"

I shrugged. "I asked one of the managers backstage. She mentioned it."

I didn't tell him about how I had cornered Gillian's stage manager after Maggie left the room. How I'd given her the third degree about Maggie Sharp and the other opening acts and had discovered it wasn't just a one-night thing but a multi-state mini-tour to promote the soundtrack for the movie. The studio was using the music to create buzz as much as anything else.

I knew what Benny was thinking. This was probably the first time I'd shown the slightest interest in any promotional tactics. I did the bare minimum—everyone knew that —and did it barely sober too.

But as soon as Maggie left the dressing room, this panic swept through me. This feeling like if I didn't see her again, never touched her again, any chance I had at escaping this shitty cycle would evaporate.

I needed more conversations than just the one from

behind the screen. More than just a single touch, hand to hand. More than a few kisses, even if they were the kind that stopped the world from turning. I needed to see if this girl, this connection, was everything it seemed.

"I want to go with them," I said. "And then they could come with us internationally too. London, Paris, Venice. All the stops." I tapped my foot impatiently. The idea of traveling the world with Maggie seemed like a fucking great idea. I knew I'd have to eat some crow about the whole Fitz Baker lie, but I wasn't ready for her to know. Not then. After, though...hell, I'd attend every damn premiere on the planet if I had her to hold my hand. "Come on. I don't have anything lined up right now."

"Except rehab."

I scowled. Benny didn't even look away. That was the real reason he was my manager—he was the only person who wasn't afraid of my glare.

"Don't even with me right now," he said. He checked around to make sure no one was listening, then scooted closer so he could speak lower. "Four hours ago, you could barely make it into the hotel. And now you're telling me you're going cold turkey on your own while you tour with a bunch of musicians? Fuck that. I love you, man, but we talked about this. You need to straighten out."

"I can do that on my own," I argued as the house lights started to drop. "I don't need a bunch of quacks coaching me through it. I've already done it once."

Benny opened his mouth to argue with me, but something else clearly occurred to him. "Who's the girl?"

I blinked but couldn't quite maintain eye contact. "Who said there was a girl?"

For that, I got an eye roll as he set his drink down on the table. "Motherfucker, how long have I known you?"

I twisted my mouth around. "I don't know. Six, seven years."

"Try ten. The one time you ever made this kind of major change in your life was with Amy. And since she left, things have been a shit show. So I'm going to ask again: who's the girl?"

The lights dimmed completely, casting my friend's face in shadow. The ice in his glass clinked as the crowd hushed, and he took a drink.

"Fine," I admitted. "You want to know who she is?"

Benny nodded.

I jerked my head toward the stage. "She's about to come on."

My manager's mouth dropped, but before he could answer, the crowd erupted in applause as several musicians walked onto the stage. Three were older, grizzly looking men who took their places at the drums, the bass guitar, and an electric. Behind them walked a woman that I would have known anywhere, despite the fact that this was the first time I'd actually seen anything besides her silhouetted profile.

I had assumed she would be beautiful. I'd seen the shape of her legs, her slender arms, her profile through the screen.

But none of those literal shadows could have prepared me for what I was looking at now.

For a moment, I couldn't breathe.

Maggie walked to the center of the stage, petite but strong in a short blue dress that revealed toned legs in a pair of cowboy boots. Her skin, a tawny brown, glowed under the lights along with the other parts of her silhouette made real—full lips pursed, glossy waves gathered over one shoulder, a small nose just turned up at the end, and dark eyes that sparked with curiosity and fear, even from this far away.

I snorted. In the blue dress, she did sort of recall a hipster Loretta Lynn, as promised. But way, way hotter. No, not hot. Goddess-level beautiful.

"He—hello," she said nervously as she stepped up to the microphone. Her low, slightly husky voice vibrated through my chest. "I'm Maggie Sharp."

"Well, I can't fault your taste," Benny muttered as we both sat forward, leaning over the balcony to get a better view. "The girl is fine. I'll give you that."

"Shut up."

I knew he didn't mean anything by it, but I couldn't help the bark. For whatever reason, even the suggestion that another man might be looking at Maggie the way I was right now made me want to hurt something. Someone.

Whoa.

"Easy," Benny said. "So, when did you meet her?"

"When I was backstage." I could barely answer. I couldn't take my eyes off her while she adjusted her microphone.

"Backstage? As in just now?"

I nodded. "We talked for about an hour while she got ready. She has stage fright. Doesn't like crowds."

"So, you have something in common," Benny said dryly.

"We have a lot more than that."

"Damn," Benny muttered, more to himself at this point than to me. "You really got hit by the arrow, didn't you?"

I didn't answer, too overtaken with concern. Maggie was nervous. Really nervous. It was in her posture, the curve of her shoulders, the way she fiddled with the microphone stand, the way she cringed with the screech echoed through the room.

"Sorry about that," she said. "H-hot mic."

"Amateur," someone muttered behind me.

I barely managed not to punch them in the face.

God. I wanted to go down there with her. Sit on the stage with her, draw some of the attention she so clearly wasn't used to. I hated it too, but I knew how to deal with it. Knew how to flash a smile at the right people, dazzle with idiotic grins and snarky statements. I wanted to tell her she didn't need to do this if she didn't want. Or else she could just pretend they were all gone, and she could just sing to me while I held her hand like I promised.

God, I wanted her to sing to me.

"Ready?" the drummer called.

Maggie glanced back with a shy smile and nodded. The drummer counted off the band with his sticks. The crowd hushed as the other musicians began to play. She was accompanied by some talent, that was for sure—seasoned old guys who had seen a show or two.

Then she stepped up to the microphone. Opened her mouth.

And absolutely nothing came out.

The musicians kept going for several seconds, but eventually, the music died away. Dread lodged in my chest while I watched her flush. I could practically feel the heat rising up her neck. Suddenly, my palms were clammy, just like I imagined hers were.

I leaned over the edge of the balcony. She wouldn't be able to see me up here. Not with the stage lights shining toward her. I knew what it was like on a stage like that. You could feel the energy of the crowd, but you couldn't see much more than the people right in the front. Everyone else was just faceless forms, bobbing shapes in a sea of shadows and lights.

But in the awkward silence, you could hear them. You could hear every whistle, every shout until they all started to blend together into a single roar.

I cupped my hands around my mouth, and before I knew it, I was standing and shouting as loud as I could, "Come on, Maggie! You got this, beautiful!"

Her head jerked, and then she was gazing straight up at me—right along with every other head in the VIP section. Her eyes darted around. She was searching for someone visible, but she couldn't see me. Not through the glare of the spotlight hanging just below where I sat.

But she wasn't alone. I wanted her to know that. So I stuck two fingers into my mouth and whistled as loud as I possibly could.

"Come on, Maggie!" I bellowed again. "Play 'The Lonely'!"

She looked like the most beautiful deer in headlights. But then, at last, there it was. A tug of a smile on the right side of her mouth. Some recognition of who was calling her name.

She said something to the drummer, who nodded. Then she turned around and spoke back into the microphone.

"Sorry about that, everyone," she said, low but somehow surer than before. "We're going to start things a little differently. This is called 'The Lonely.' For the fan in the crowd."

Once more, the drummer counted them off. The bassist started with a line as insistent as a train, followed by riffs from the rhythm guitarist that slithered in like snakes. Lastly, Maggie started to strum her acoustic guitar, lending fullness to the layers that were less decipherable but somehow just as necessary to the entire equation.

There were a few more cheers from the crowd while the band drove its steady rhythm harder. Energy was rising in the club. The hairs on the back of my neck stood up.

Then Maggie began to sing.

And the entire world—the lights, the cameras, the crowds—all of it just melted away.

I was born to hear this woman make music.

ELEVEN

Maggie

I was drenched with sweat when I got back to my dressing room, fatigued and anxious at the same time. My heart was still pounding hard enough I could feel it in my ears, right behind the roar of the crowd and the echoes of the sound system still blaring as the next band took the stage. I was going to have to invest in some earplugs. There was a reason so many musicians had hearing loss.

"Holy crap, girl! That was a damn show and a half! You killed it!"

I whirled around to find Calliope bursting through the door with a triumphant grin.

"Cal! Oh, Christ, you scared me." I pressed a hand to my chest but couldn't help returning the smile.

My best friend tipped her head. Her braids swayed over her shoulder. "I always meet you in the back. Where else were you expecting me to be?"

"I don't know. I think I'm still high on the show."

I shook my head as I made for the bag of clothes I'd

left at the far end of the room. My dress was pasted on me like a second skin. It was a short set, but I was still drenched. Only fifteen minutes as the opener, followed by the other two bands, and then Gillian's full set. My hair was soaked all around my hairline and on the back of my neck. I held it up to allow the cool air to provide some relief, then collapsed into the chair and pulled off my boots.

"Oh, God, that feels good," I groaned as I wriggled my toes.

"I'm not surprised," Calliope said as she leaned against the top of the vanity next to me. "I don't think I've ever seen you move like that around the stage."

I glanced up at her playfully. "What are you saying?"

"What do you think I'm saying? You were like another woman up there, my friend, and I don't mean that in a bad way. I've always sold you as a songwriter, not a performer. But tonight? Girl, you were the whole package."

I couldn't take offense at Calliope's insinuation that, in my heart, I wasn't actually a true performer. She was right. I'd always loathed getting on stage. It usually took me more than one song to get lost in my music, and even then, it required extreme focus. Anxiety was a killer.

Tonight, too. It almost got me.

When the band had launched into that first song, it was like the sound check all over again. Only this time, there was a crowd in front of me. I was literally blinded by the lights, and my voice turned to ice. Even the microphone shrieked like it wanted me off the stage.

I had truly been about to run off in a blind terror when I heard his voice echoing from the rafters.

Come on, Maggie!

Hoarse but deep. Familiar, like the warm fingers that

had encircled my wrist. The icy constriction around my throat had loosened, and I knew what to do.

So, on the spur of the moment, I changed the song order. George counted us off.

I could have sworn that even through the glare of the stage lights, two other bright sparks gleamed from the balcony. Eager and kind. And so I opened my mouth and sang to them.

"Seriously," Calliope pushed. "What got into you? Or was it just the fact that you had a fan here tonight?"

I frowned until I realized she was talking about him. My stranger. "I—I don't know. I was just inspired, I guess."

I could have told her then. Knowing Callie, she probably would have run right back to the VIP section to interrogate every person up there until she found the identity of my mysterious company. She'd probably bully him into coming to every show I had after this.

But for whatever reason, I wasn't ready to say it out loud yet. My heart rate was finally returning to normal, but as soon as I checked the clock above the door, it picked right back up again. He'd promised to come after my show. And right now, covered in sweat, I probably looked closer to a creature from the black lagoon than the cute girl he was hoping to see.

If he had liked what he'd seen at all.

"I need to clean up," I said, standing. "Half my makeup melted out there. I look like a used candle."

"I'll wait. We need to talk."

"There's a chair behind the screen if you want to sit. Or the couch," I said as I pulled my dress over my head. Considering we'd shared a room for almost four years, I was used to changing in front of Callie.

"So, get this. It wasn't just me that was impressed,

babe," she said as I pulled out the jeans and T-shirt I had packed, plus the bag of makeup and toiletries that would help me look halfway presentable. "I had four A&R reps approach me during your set. Four! Plus one Theo del Conte."

I pressed a couple of makeup wipes over my face. "Who's that?"

"'Who's that?'" Callie parroted. "The only son of Maximilian del Conte, remember? The one who had eyes for you before the show. That's Del Conte Entertainment, babe. They are giving Sony and Time Warner a run for their money since the merger with that Chinese studio. And according to a little bird, Daddy del Conte is giving his little boy control of the music department."

I blinked as I turned back to the mirror, then drew the wipe over my eyelids, trying to clean up the remnants of the heavy stage makeup. I looked like a raccoon. "I'll take your word for it. You follow that stuff, not me."

Callie continued to rattle on about the Del Contes and their importance. Per usual, the industry speak was breezing over my head. I just wanted to write music. And, if it could be like this all the time, maybe I could perform too.

I couldn't help glancing through the mirror in the direction of the screen, like my stranger was still there, ready to give me another pep talk. Truthfully, the idea that he was out there had made all the difference. I had heard his velvety voice humming along with mine. Envisioned his strong, warm hands on my waist every time I stepped or swayed. For the first time on stage, I hadn't felt alone. I was lifted up. And clearly, it had shown.

Maybe, in a few minutes, I'd meet him for real. See the face that matched the voice.

My heartbeat picked up once more as suddenly, I

wanted Callie out of here as soon as possible. I wasn't ready to reveal the reason for my change. Not yet. Not before I had even met my savior for real.

First, I needed to look presentable. So while Callie jabbered about the different people who were apparently begging to sign me now, I didn't even stop to think about why the prospect of meeting my stranger excited me more than the possibility of my music career finally getting its break. I just put on my clean clothes—simple jeans and a T-shirt—and set about fixing my unruly hair and makeup into something that was less stage-girl and more me. Simple. Plain, even.

But genuine.

For a moment, I wondered if that was a mistake. After all, the stranger had already watched me sing, made up in my dress, with the dark eyes and lipstick and perfect hair that Callie had insisted on. Maybe that's what he was hoping to meet again when he came back.

No, a voice said inside.

If he couldn't deal with me this way, he couldn't deal with me at all. And something deep down told me this was the sort of man who cared a lot more about what was on the inside than out.

"Hey, are these yours?"

I turned to find Callie emerging from behind the screen, not with the chair, but instead with what looked like a prescription bottle and an empty plastic bag.

Or almost empty. When she handed them to me, I saw a small blue pill at the bottom of the bag. Unlabeled, seemingly innocuous.

But only one kind of pill was usually found at the bottom of a sandwich bag. The kind that wasn't supposed to be taken.

"Tricia Owens?" I murmured as I turned the bottle over and back.

As far as I knew, no one else had been using this dressing room tonight, but that didn't mean no one had been here while I was on stage. Or this wasn't from the night before. Or maybe while I had been upstairs with my guitar.

Right?

"I cleaned this room myself before you," Calliope answered my unspoken questions. "This wasn't here before we got here."

A finger of something cold slid down my back as I stared at the bottle. It didn't mean it was his. They could belong to someone in another band, although I happened to know none of them included a person named Tricia. Deep down, I knew the truth. Matching name or not, these had belonged to the man behind the screen. I had heard something rattling while he sat back there, which I could now clearly identify as pills in a plastic container.

I passed the bottle and bag back to Calliope. "Can you get rid of these, please?"

She nodded without question. She knew exactly how I felt about things like this. I had a mother at home who couldn't handle her booze. Her struggles with sobriety had cost me so much already—including the knowledge of who my father was. I wanted nothing to do with drugs, addiction, anything like it.

Even for a voice who pulsed through a crowd, whose touch calmed me like a cool summer breeze.

"Let's go," I said.

"Go? We can't go. You've got a line of reps waiting so see you after Gillian's set. We need to stick around.

Networking, babe. It's going to make your career, I promise."

I sighed. Shit, she was right.

But before I could answer, the door flew open, and one of the club's security detail blew in.

"Hey girls," he said. "Time to go."

Calliope crossed her arms and frowned. "What? Why?"

"There's a mob out there right now. I'm serious, ladies. You need to get out before they charge the stage."

We both looked over the big man's shoulder, like we expected to see said mob entering the dressing room right at that moment. They didn't, of course, but it was then I realized that the low roar emitting from the direction of the stage was no longer overlaid with constant drumbeats or the strum of guitars. Just shouting, screaming. Chaos.

My arms were suddenly covered in goose bumps. One look at Callie told me she was feeling the same way.

"What's going on?" she asked, her low voice nearly a whisper. "What happened?"

"A fight," the bouncer said tersely. "Down in the pit. Some asshole from the VIP section started pushing people around. I don't know who." He glanced behind him. "Get your stuff, ladies. We need to get everyone out the back before the cops show up."

And with that, he was gone. I stood there, bumbling, while Calliope started rushing around, making sure my stuff was packed up.

"It's just the one guitar, right?" she said.

"Well, the two others were still in the wings—"

"I'll make sure the club owner stores them," Calliope said, already tapping out a message on her phone.

"But—" I started.

"But what?"

"But, the meetings," I said feebly, though I was already putting my clothes into my bag, albeit slowly. I didn't know how to say it. That I was waiting for a man I'd never met. That he probably wouldn't come until after the show was over, and that despite the pills we'd found, I was still desperate to see the face that belonged to that voice.

"I have their numbers, Maggie. Come on! You heard the man."

"But—"

Callie grabbed my wrist, jerking my attention to her. "Maggie. Do you hear that?"

I shut my mouth. The roar outside had intensified far beyond the average concert fare. Sounds of breaking glass and the occasional shout were now filtering through and getting louder. There was no music. Only the rumble of feet.

"That doesn't sound like a fight, Maggie. It's a riot." Calliope took her purse off the counter and grabbed my arm. "I'm not interested in being a couple of brown girls trapped in a broom closet by a mob of drunk country fans. We need to scram. Like, yesterday."

A scream filtered through. More shouts. A loud crash, like a table had been broken.

No one was coming back here for us. At least not anyone we'd want to see.

I looked at the pills still sitting on the edge of the dressing room table.

Maybe it was for the best.

"All right," I said, springing into action. "Yeah, let's get out of here."

TWELVE

Will

"Turn."

The sergeant's voice was gruff and scratchy, like a Brillo pad over silver. Obediently, I turned while the small camera perched above the station's computer flashed.

"To the front."

Again, I obeyed and stared blankly into the camera. Well, as best I could, with one eye nearly swollen shut. Yeah, this wasn't exactly the photo op I was expecting today. My hair was sticking up on one side after being stuffed into a squad car. I had the stains of who knew how many drinks splattered across my T-shirt, and if my puffy eyelid was any indicator, the beginnings of a solid shiner were forming above my left cheekbone. By this time tomorrow, someone in this station would have made a quick fifty grand selling this exact picture to the most eager tabloid. Within twenty-four hours, it would be all over the news. You couldn't count on much in the world, but grifters were always around.

I could see the headlines now, splashed right over my mug shot.

Another fight for Fitz Baker

Fitz's fists land him in jail

Jailbird Baker—*Will* he ever reform?

"Follow me," said the officer with a curt nod toward the back of the station. "I'd give you your own cell, but we're full up tonight. Lotsa trouble-makers out there."

Like you.

He didn't need to say it out loud. I heard it anyway.

"Say, listen," he said, pausing at the door to the jail. "I was wondering…"

I turned with a barely masked scowl. He wasn't really going to do this while he was escorting me to a jail cell, was he?

"My daughter, she's a huge fan," the officer continued. "Used to watch reruns of *Bailey's Life* every night at five."

Jesus. He was doing this. He really was.

He pulled nervously on his goatee as he continued. "You, ah, wouldn't mind signing an autograph for her, would you? I only see her on the weekends, right, and it would go a long way next time I see her."

And there it was. Proof solid that everyone had an angle. And what was I supposed to do? Say no to the guy getting ready to lock me up, even if it was just for twenty minutes?

I sighed. I had a self-destructive streak, but I was tapped out tonight. "Sure. Anything for fans."

The sergeant produced an index card and a pen from

his back pocket—clearly, he'd been thinking about this since he booked me. I signed the same unintelligible scrawl I'd been using since I was maybe twelve or thirteen, then handed it back to him.

"You, uh, you mind a picture too? She'll never believe I met you."

Sure. Because booking someone is the beginning of the most beautiful friendship, isn't it?

"I'm not really in the best place for a photo," I said, gesturing around toward the concrete hall.

"Oh, she won't mind. My girl's your biggest fan, I tell you."

It was one thing to sign a card, but it was another to memorialize the whole experience against this cold concrete wall and the hallway that smelled like piss and drying out drunks.

"Sorry," I said tightly. "The answer's no."

The sergeant's doughy face immediately transformed into a scowl. "You joking? You can't take one picture for my little girl?"

But now I was immovable. "Well, you already got one picture tonight, Serg. Just make a copy of my mug shot."

Apparently, I was completely out of fucks. The night was already completely ruined. What did I care if I irritated the guy? What was he going to do? Arrest me again?

The sergeant eyed me for a moment longer, then, without a word, pushed by me to unlock the door to the jail and lead me down a hall toward the cells for minor arrests. People who would either wait to be bailed out or for a possible transfer to a bigger detention facility while they awaited trial. I shivered. I'd never get that far.

"Enjoy your night," he sneered as he opened the door to

a cell where more than one occupant was eyeing me with curiosity and recognition.

I saluted, but before I could say, "Will do," we were interrupted by another cop.

"Meier! Wait!"

We both turned to find another officer walking down the hall with a clip-clop of boots on vinyl.

"His attorney just showed up," she said once she caught us. "Paid his bond. He's good to go."

I grinned at the sergeant, who just looked even more annoyed he couldn't say he locked up Fitz Baker.

"Sorry, man," I told him as I stepped around to follow the policewoman. "I'm sure there'll be a next time."

I followed her back to the reception desk, where I found Benny pacing near a row of orange bench seats.

"What took you so long?" I demanded.

He whirled around, causing his loosened tie to fly up in his face.

"You owe me five hundred bucks. And what's the problem? Pretty boy couldn't deal with five minutes in the slammer?" Benny's voice was more than irritated. "I got here as fast as I could. Wasn't easy—there's another fuckin' riot outside the station."

I looked over his shoulder. The windows were tinted, but I could already imagine the uproar crowding the sidewalk outside the precinct. "Fuck."

"Paps followed the squad car," Benny answered the unspoken question. "And the fans?"

"Followed the paps," I supplied. It was the same everywhere. Right now, though, I wasn't sure I could take it.

"Don't worry," he said. "One of the officers said you could take the back way out."

Another favor. But nothing's free.

"Who, another donut-loving sergeant? What did he want in return, a lock of hair?"

"Stop complaining, Will. You sound like more of a dick than usual. In fact, you sound like a damn spoiled brat. Just try, for a fucking second, to show some gratitude."

I opened my mouth to argue but found I couldn't. Benny didn't usually go off at me like that. In fact, he tolerated my bullshit better than most. But every now and then, I'd get a little too much, and all it took was a quick word from my best friend to pull me back to, well, if not reality, something closer than this life of mine typically afforded.

"Fine," I said. "And thanks. Where do we go, then?"

"This way."

I followed him around the front desk, flashing a smile through my bruises at the officers sitting at their desks until we ducked down another hall that led to a back alley. With any luck, we'd be limited to two, maybe three photographers at most. A hell of a lot better than the main pack.

Just as we reached the exit, though, Benny's phone rang.

"Hold up," he called to me. "Shit."

I turned near the exit. "What? What is it?"

Benny didn't say anything, just handed me his phone. And there I was, a full twenty-four hours earlier than I predicted. My gorgeous mug in its purple and blue glory, staring into the camera with the glare that *US Weekly* called my "broody pantymelter." I still wasn't convinced my mother didn't pay for that feature. Either way, it was embarrassing as fuck.

I scrolled down through the article. The usual garbage. Fitz Baker getting into a fight, drinking too much. Shit about Amelia and me. Speculation that I wasn't on something beyond alcohol. I'd seen it all before.

But after scrolling through and back up again, I caught

an image that I hadn't seen previously. No, not an image. A video. Of me.

The internet is forever, my friends. That's the truth.

There I was, pushing through the crowd like some kind of insane animal. In another, taking a swing at some guy while another tried to hold me back. Whirling around when someone tried to tap me on the shoulder, getting shoved in one direction, and immediately throwing myself back at whoever I perceived had done it.

From there, the fight was a ripple through the crowd. People were thrown into other people, more fist fighting broke out until someone screamed, and suddenly the entire crowd started to barge toward one of the exits. Over the sound system, I could hear Gillian Jacobs trying desperately to calm everyone down until, finally, she gave up.

In the center of it all was still me, flying off the handle, wreathed in the rage that took over the second I couldn't get to Maggie.

It was bad. Really bad. Even worse because, to be honest, I wasn't sure I was even sorry for what had happened. Maybe for breaking that guy's nose. Maybe for causing the riot that sent the other one to the hospital. But for trying to get to Maggie? I wasn't sure I'd ever be sorry for that.

Not that it mattered now. She was long gone.

"Well, it's done," I said, handing the phone back to Benny.

"The car is waiting outside off Eleventh," he said as he tucked the phone away. "Another is out front ready to act as a decoy."

I nodded. It was a shell game we played all the time.

"Trish said she'd talk to Corden and Meyers. Make sure they don't ask you about tonight."

I jerked. "Why?"

Benny just looked apologetic. "You know she's the best at this shit."

"At what? Cleaning up my messes?"

He didn't answer.

"She knows how to sweet talk the networks and the press when it comes to you," Benny continued. "You have three late-night appearances this week, a West Coast junket, and four major profiles scheduled. They're gonna ask about tonight. I can't stop them. But your mom, maybe she can."

I growled. "Maybe we should just tell the damn truth for once."

"Do *you* want to explain why you almost burned down Irving Plaza just to chase a girl?"

I opened my mouth to say *fuck them, sure,* but then immediately closed it once it occurred to me what he was getting at. If anything about Maggie got out in any way, the paps would be on her like flies on shit. She'd be suffocated completely, pilloried on social media, stalked by the press. Everyone would want to know who Fitz Baker's new girl was.

And I couldn't do that to her. Shit, I wouldn't wish that on anyone.

"Fine," I grumbled. "She can help. But I'm *not* signing her for shit."

Benny just nodded and started again toward the back exit of the station. Just before we reached the door, though, his phone rang again.

"Speak of the devil." He held up the device bearing my mother's name, then answered. "Hey—whoa, Trish. Slow down. What happened?"

He listened for a minute or so, and I watched my

friend's eyes grow wider every second through nervous glances my way.

"What is it?" I asked. I could hear my mother's frantic shrilling but couldn't make out what she was saying.

Benny just held up a hand while he listened.

"All right," he said finally. "Yeah, okay. We're on our way." He ended the call. "Change of plans. We're going to Stamford."

I frowned. "Why? What's going on?"

"God, I'm so—I'm so sorry, man. It's Michael, he's in the hospital. Will, your dad just had a heart attack."

THIRTEEN

Will

An hour later, I found myself right back where I had been earlier that day—sitting on the deck of the shabby blue house, staring across acres of wetlands toward the Long Island Sound.

Benny had driven me straight to the hospital from the jail, only for us to be turned away. Visiting hours at the ICU were over, and only spouses were allowed at night—not an autograph or cash could sway the on-call nurse's mind. I had to respect her for it. There aren't many people in this world who aren't moved by fame or money. But it also meant I'd have to wait until morning to see my dad.

Mom was there now, though she didn't plan to stay the night with him. It made me despise her even more. For some reason, I couldn't help thinking of Maggie in comparison. I barely knew the girl, but I had a feeling she wasn't the type who would choose a cozy hotel over an ICU chair when her husband was in the hospital. She seemed pretty damn ride or die to me.

But what did I know from just a kiss?

I looked out to the water, glossy and deep, with only a few lines shining visibly on the other side of its immense blackness. Maggie would like it here, I'd bet. She wouldn't laugh at the idea of me being a fisherman's son or wrinkle her nose at the brackish mix of the wetlands and Dad's fishing equipment.

I touched my hand to my mouth. It was the dream of that touch, that body, that *mouth* that had driven me out into that crowd like a madman.

I'd originally planned to wait until the end of the show to find her, just like we'd said. At first, it had seemed tenable. The two acts that followed her had similarly short sets, though each of their fifteen minutes had seemed like hours compared to hers. She'd been nervous when she started, but then she'd sung to me—I *knew* she was singing to me. And her talent blew everyone out of the water.

By the time the headliner started, though, I was done waiting. It took me another hour, I swear, to extricate myself from the collection of agents, studio executives, handlers, and other people who were all dying to meet me that night. Even Benny didn't want me to go, convinced I was only leaving to find a new fix.

I was, in a way. As soon as Maggie had walked into that dressing room, drugs were the last thing on my mind, and at the time, I had been determined to keep it that way.

Now, though, I wasn't so sure. Maybe that was part of why I'd gone so nuts.

After finding both entrances to the backstage stairs locked from the VIP level, I'd been too impatient to ask Benny to help me find the manager of the place. Instead, I'd decided to take the path of least resistance to the stage area: straight through the crowd.

No one would notice, right?

Wrong.

I squeezed my eyes closed. Now my body was yowling, demanding *something* to take the edge off—and it wasn't that different from the crazed need that had driven me through all those people. That made me knock a guy out cold when he had thought to push me out of his way. That had caused me to start ramming myself into the crowd like a fool.

The more I did, the harder they fought. The more they fought, the more insane the crowd grew until it was nothing but brawling bodies and shouts and crunching bones.

I'd never seen or felt anything like it. Pure insanity.

And still, I couldn't get to her. Not before the cops came. Not before three people were taken away in an ambulance. Not before I was cuffed alongside two other assholes and carted off to the Thirteenth Precinct station.

The pounding deepened. My skin felt like it was separating itself from my muscle and bone. I wanted to crawl inside myself, but nothing seemed like the right fix anymore. Not pills. Not weed. Not drink. Not anything Benny could provide. And Maggie? Maggie was long gone by now, if she'd ever stayed in the first place.

The water, though. That seemed pretty damn inviting.

"He's just out here, Trish."

I didn't turn at the sound of the screen door opening.

"Mom," I said as my mother came to stand next to me. I didn't look up. Her pristine patent shoes were practically mirrors. "Any news?"

When I looked up, I was unsurprised to find her seething. My mother seethed a lot. I was, however, surprised it was directed at me.

"*What* are you doing?" she demanded.

I reeled. "What does it look like I'm doing?"

"My God, Will. How can you just sit there and act like nothing has happened?"

I blinked. Was she for real with this? "What are you talking about? What am I supposed to do? We tried to get into the ICU, but Nurse Ratched said only you could stay, so we came here to wait. Look, it's not my fault that Dad had a heart attack."

"You're damn right it's your fault!" she shouted. "My husband is in the hospital fighting for his life right now because *you* put him there, you ungrateful brat!"

At that, I pushed myself up to standing. It took everything I had not to sway.

The screen door opened, and Benny poked his head outside. "Ah, everything all right out here? And may I remind you that Michael has some very curious neighbors? Some of which would probably be more than happy to sell anything they hear to TMZ?"

"Me?" I demanded without any care for my manager or his warnings. "Can you explain how I'm somehow responsible for this mess when I wasn't anywhere near him?"

"It's very simple, Fitzwilliam." My mother's voice dropped considerably, though it was still dripping with contempt. "You did what you always do. Fell into a wormhole of drugs and sex and God only knows what else, lost control, and took it out on everyone else around you like a child having a tantrum. Only this time, you actually got into some trouble for it. *This* time you actually ended up arrested, and this time I was with him, Will."

"Horseshit," I countered immediately. "You weren't with him. You were in New York with us, schmoozing it up, using your famous kid to bag your next client."

I glanced at Benny for confirmation. He looked like he would rather be anywhere else.

"Ah, Trish left right after the photocall at Irving Plaza. She didn't stay for the show."

"That's right," Mom spat. "I had to come back here and talk some things over. Money things. The house needs a new roof, for one." When she caught my stupefied expression, she smirked. "What, you never wondered how your father could maintain a property like this?"

"This place was never that nice," I said. "Dad kept it because it was the one thing that ever belonged to him."

My mother looked at me like I was completely simple. "Fitzwilliam, did it never occur to you that even fifteen years ago, your father couldn't have possibly afforded the taxes on a waterfront property an hour from New York on a fisherman's salary? It was your father's choice to keep it like this."

She waved her hand backward, as if to indicate the general upkeep of the property. I followed and rolled my eyes. The house wasn't in bad shape. Dad was actually always fanatical about keeping the lawn mowed, the gutters cleaned, the shingles in good order, and repainting at least twice since I was a kid. It was a little weather-worn, and yeah, it stood out on a street that had been half-rebuilt with new Cape Cods. But she acted like it was a hovel. It wasn't.

"But it still took money," she finished. "Mostly money."

Her money. Made mostly off me. Which meant *my* money.

I turned back to her, unable to conceal my surprise. Dad always said that my career was my own. It had never occurred to me that he would have taken a single dollar I'd ever earned for himself.

And yet, here I was. Standing on the evidence of it.

I shook off the fact. I had more than enough to share with my old man or anyone else who needed it.

"It doesn't matter," I said. "And fine. So you were here to give your husband some cash. I still don't know what the hell that has to do with me."

The fury returned to her face. Somewhere, deep down, I wondered if my mother still loved my father on some level. Why else would she be upset?

"It has to do with the fact that the moment he saw his precious boy's face on that television brawling like a two-bit criminal, your father's heart gave out," she said in a voice that was both deadly and strong. "It has to do with the fact that you—you—" She wrung her hands like she'd just washed something horrible from them and was trying to dry them out. "If he dies tonight, Fitzwilliam, it will be because *you* killed him!"

I reared back like I'd been slapped. Benny took that moment to step out fully onto the porch.

"Trish," he said as he reached my side. "Come on, that's unfair."

"A father can only take so much stress from his children," Mom snapped at him. "One of these days Will is going to kill his. If he hasn't already."

And with that, she strode back into the house, slamming the screen door behind her and leaving me to slump back to the ground. Everything forgotten but the words ringing inside my head like the innards of a bell.

Ding. Ding.

On and on it rang, resonant and full.

Ding. Ding.

Dad. Dad.

I collapsed forward. My body ached. Sweat was

building on my skin, causing my clothes to stick. My skin prickled all over, suddenly hot and cold at the same time.

I needed...fucking hell, I didn't even know what.

I scratched my arm, an itch that wouldn't fade. There was another one at my shoulder. Behind my ear. I didn't want any more pills. I didn't. But right now, they were the first thing on my mind. Not my dad. Not Maggie. Just tracking down another orange bottle.

"Fuck," I whispered.

"Hey."

I barely registered Benny sinking down to the porch step next to me, apparently disregarding the effect of unswept wood on his designer suit.

"She's wrong, man," he said, setting a hand on my shoulder. "Michael is in the hospital because of unlucky genetics and a lifetime of eating bacon for every breakfast. Not because of you."

"She's right," I insisted. "If he dies tonight, it will be because I killed him." I scratched viciously at my knees, then clenched them hard enough that I could feel my fingernails through the denim.

"You need something?"

I gritted my teeth. "I thought you weren't going to be my dealer anymore."

He looked sorry for me. It made me that much angrier. That much more desperate.

"I'd make an exception for tonight. Anyone would need a little something to get through this shit. Besides, two weeks, man. One short tour, and you're back in rehab. I'd rather you get what you need from me than some asshole on the street who might land you in the hospital."

The thought of the press tour made me physically ill. Nausea lurched through my stomach, and suddenly I realized it wasn't a passing phase. I jumped up and barely made it to the edge of the porch before I emptied the contents of my stomach—which wasn't much at that point of the evening—into the reeds and bushes on the other side.

Benny just watched without judgment. But he didn't offer me anything else.

I turned, wiping my heated face with the back of my hand. My bones hurt. My entire body hurt. But all I could think was one thing.

"*Fuck*, Benny. I wish it were me. I should have had the fucking heart attack, not him. He could die. And it should have been me."

"You don't want to be dead, my friend," Benny said. "I know you don't."

"Maybe it would be better if I was," I whispered.

"Don't talk like that."

It was an order, not a suggestion.

Benny had been with me through everything. Through the times I had actually contemplated suicide, just after Amy left. Through more than one minor overdose. Through two other trips to rehab. Right now, though, there was a fear in his voice I had never heard before.

Maybe because it matched the sorrow in mine.

My. Fault.

I teetered back toward the step and sank back down next to my friend. "I can't do this anymore, Ben."

"I know. Which is why, right after the press tour, we're going to get you back into rehab, man. Get you sober and healthy again—"

"I have *never* been healthy," I interrupted. "And I don't just mean physically. I mean this. This life. All of it. I can't do it anymore."

There was a long silence.

"Will, you're not saying you want to…"

Fear threaded through my friend's voice once again as he drifted off, unable to voice what he was really thinking. Maybe because he was scared of putting ideas in my mind.

Too late.

I shook my head as, for some reason, the girl from the show, Maggie—her face interrupted those dark thoughts. A bit of warmth in the middle of this icy reality.

I blinked her away. That dream was long gone. But its memory had a real effect.

"No," I said. "I don't want to kill myself. But maybe—" I took a deep breath. "Maybe everyone else needs to think I did."

I could practically hear Benny gulp beside me. He was searching for the way to tell me I was out of my mind.

But I turned, suddenly full of resolve. "No, I'm serious. We could do this. I can disappear, make it look like I died. Killed myself, whatever. People can mourn. Hero worship, whatever they want. Heroes are always better to people when they're dead, anyway. That way, they can't fuck up the story."

"But, but," Benny sputtered. "Will, you can't *die*! That's insane!"

"Well, if you send me back out there, I'll die anyway. You know I will. Look at me, man. You *know*, I will. I already came close to killing my father. Who knows, maybe he is dead already. Two other people almost died tonight. If you aren't feeding me pills, I'll probably end up on a gurney anyway with something I find elsewhere. Who else am I going to hurt, huh? I want out, Ben. For myself and for everyone else around me. Please."

Benny stared at me for a long time, searching my face

for any sign of delirium, high, anything that suggested I wasn't thinking straight.

But I was sober now. Enough to know exactly what I was saying.

"You can do it, Ben," I pressed. "You can help me. Consider it your last act as my agent. But I know you can. You'll tell everyone whatever they need to hear to believe it. Please, man. I'm begging you. Haven't I given you and everyone else enough?"

He opened his mouth, clearly ready to argue another round. But he must have seen something in my eyes that made him stop. He knew I was serious. And when I was like this, there was no changing my mind.

"It will take me a minute," he said after a while.

I grinned. This was why Benny was the best manager around. He could make anything happen. Even if it was the craziest thing anyone ever asked for.

"We'd have to start with power of attorney," he said. "You can't just pretend to jump off a bridge, man. Something like this?" He shook his head, like he couldn't even believe what he was saying.

"Anything," I promised. "You say, I do."

He snorted. "Because you've always been the obedient type." Nonetheless, he kept going, brain whirring with possibilities. "We'd have to move your money around, make it look like you're broke or something, or close to it. Leave enough for Trish and Michael to inherit as your next of kin, move the rest to untraceable accounts. Swiss, probably. You've already got some in the Caymans, but that's a little shady. I'll get an LLC up in Delaware for US property transactions. You've got plenty of money, but that will be the trail most people follow."

"Whatever you say."

It was a little weird to trust someone this much with my assets, but I couldn't have cared less about them at this point. I just wanted to disappear. If my money made that harder, then he could throw it in the bottom of the ocean for all I cared.

"Are you really sure about this?" he asked midway through his brainstorming. "You could just retire and hole up in Vermont. People do it all the time. They leave Hollywood and start new lives. That girl from the *Wonder Years*. Frankie Muniz. Shit, that kid from *A Christmas Story*, you know?"

But I just shook my head hard. "No one ever really fades away, Benny. People still find them somehow. All those people you mentioned, they still get reporters tracking them down, stalkers, people throwing money at them, trying to get them back in the game. No one ever really leaves the fame machine. It's death or nothing. And I don't want to die, Benny."

He worried his jaw but didn't argue. He knew as well as I did that it was true. Fame was a drug to the famous, yeah, but more to the people who followed them. Some people really felt like when you became famous, you belonged to them. And they could never let you go.

Finally, he shrugged. "I need some time. Something like this takes careful planning. If we can even pull it off."

"A month, a year, two years, whatever. I can do it, Ben. I can do whatever you need as long as I know it's waiting for me. As long as I know my family is all right." I snorted. "Maybe I should feign a heart attack too."

The joke fell flat. I thought of my dad, curled in agony on the ground. I knew enough about what a heart attack was like, if only because I'd pretended to have one in a film. Here's to research.

No, I couldn't do that.

"No, not a year. Say, a month. Maybe two or three." Benny was too busy planning to pay attention to my black humor. "You *sure* you want me to do this?"

I nodded, still entranced by the vision I had of my dad.

"Just get me the fuck out of this life, Ben." My voice cracked. "Get me out of theirs. If you don't, I'll die anyway. And next time, he might too." I shook my head. My dad would be hurt. He was the only one who really would. But I also knew I was more dangerous in his life than out of it.

I had never known anything to be truer.

And it seemed my best friend knew it too.

FOURTEEN

Maggie

"You know the rules, baby. Put it on."

I smiled at the voice behind me, full of mischief. "Why don't you put it on first?"

"Already done. It's your turn. No arguments."

My belly warmed in response to the gentle command. My stranger was back. I never knew when he would show up, but it seemed like it had been more and more frequently. In the library. The back of a cab. Once, he even cornered me at the gym.

Today, though, we had a bit more time. He'd found me in my bedroom just after I'd gotten home from another gig.

"Close your eyes," he growled behind my ear.

Obediently, I did.

"Just once, I'd like to see you. I still don't know what you look like," I said as he wrapped the soft silk around my eyes, blacking out the world around me. "Will it always be like this?"

"For now." He finished knotting my blindfold, then

turned me around, presumably to face him. "You were brilliant tonight, by the way."

"So you *have* seen me play," I said. "First at Irving Plaza, and now tonight?"

There was a low rumble in the back of his throat that I thought might have been a bit of laughter. "Maggie, I've been to every one of your shows since the Plaza."

I blinked under the silk. He'd never said. After the riot had caused her guitarist to sprain his wrist, Gillian had canceled the first few shows while he healed. I had only played a few spots at some bars and a few open mics to keep myself rehearsed before the tour began in earnest. I'd never seen anyone I'd even suspected to be him. Wouldn't I have known?

Then again, how could I have?

"What, are you stalking me?" I joked.

There was no answer. I had only just started wondering why I didn't care when his fingers threaded into my hair, then cupped the back of my head.

"Would it matter if I was?"

His lips barely brushed mine, which parted in response. He was toying with me. I craned my face up, eager for a kiss, but when he didn't grant it, I found myself shaking with frustration.

"Patience," he said as he grazed his nose up and down my jawline. The hands at the back of my head massaged my scalp lightly, then slid downward, pausing briefly around my neck, cupping my shoulders, slipping under my arms, then following my curves to my waist.

"I was born to touch you." His deep voice was a growl as his hands slipped under my shirt, then tugged it up and off.

"You were," I agreed as I did the same, finding the edges of his T-shirt and helping him take it off.

Then we were skin to skin, chest to chest, hips to hips. My fingertips grazed the muscles around his waist, enjoying the bricked structure of his abs, the sculpted plane of his chest. I didn't need to see him to know he was a work of art. This body had been imprinted on my mind for weeks through nothing but touch.

My stranger.

"Off," I insisted, yanking at the buttons of his jeans.

"Impatient today, are we?"

So said the man currently taking ample squeezes of my backside and grunting with each one.

"More every day, if you want to know the truth," I replied, pressing my nose into the soft hollow just above his collarbone.

He smelled divine. No more nicotine—just a hint of salt water, pine trees, and the tinge of a nameless cologne. I could have spent the entire evening with my nose buried right here. If, of course, he wasn't offering so much more.

"Then I'd better give you what you want."

His fingers slipped under my chin, tilting my face up. His cheek brushed mine, slight stubble to my smooth skin, drifting, drifting, until our mouths finally met.

"Fuck, *Maggie*," he growled just before his tongue tangled with mine.

I opened wide. He tasted good, *so* good—a taste I could never forget, a taste I seemed to always crave. He tasted like wanting and warmth and desire and love. He tasted like home.

Everything about him was warm as my hands wandered over his body. I trailed my fingers up and down his broad back, looking for purchase as he continued to take everything he wanted from our kiss. He walked me backward until I felt the edge of my bed under my knees. They buckled obediently, and then in the darkness of our own making, we collapsed together, my body buried in the nest of my duvet, his on top of me.

"Maggie," he murmured as his lips followed my jaw to my ear, which he proceeded to nip. "I don't want to stop this time."

"Don't," I agreed, slipping my hands down to his hips in order to help him shuck his jeans. Yes, he was warm down there too.

And then he was naked, or so I felt, as the very tip of him slipped between my legs. My stranger groaned into my shoulder.

"Please," he begged before worrying my ear between his teeth. "Please don't make me stop tonight."

Stop? When had I ever wanted him to stop? I wanted him to do this every night. I had been aching for this moment for more than a month, whimpered for it between kisses, died whenever he left me without so much as a name.

"Can we take off the blindfolds? Please?"

His big body paused on top of me. Tension stymied his action. "Why—why now?"

I swallowed, suddenly shy again. "Don't you think we ought to see each other's faces first? Before we, you know?"

He was quiet a long time, pressing his mouth into my hairline as he thought. I could still feel him hard between my legs, but he made no move forward. I had to stop myself from rocking into him. Why had I opened my big mouth?

"I'll make you a deal," he told me at last. "I'll look now. And you can see me after."

I frowned. "That doesn't seem particularly fair."

"All's fair in love and war, beautiful."

I snorted. "You don't even know if I'm beautiful—"

"Ah, but I do. Your shows, remember?"

That just made me scowl. "That's from far away."

"True."

"But if you've already seen me, then *I* should be the one to see you first, not the other way around."

He sighed. The shoulders caging mine didn't move, but I could feel his breath on my chest along with the tickle of his hair, which had grown just down to his chin.

"That's all I'm offering tonight, Maggie. Take it or leave it."

I wiggled beneath him, but he didn't move. I didn't know much about my stranger, but I knew he was infuriatingly stubborn. The man really would cut off his nose to spite his own face. Or, I assumed, not actually knowing what his stupid face looked like.

I could have wriggled out. He wouldn't have forced me. This was my choice, though with his lean body skimming mine, he wasn't exactly making it easy to walk away. Or rather, to *want* to walk away.

Once again, my stranger was proving himself much more stubborn than me.

"Fine," I grumbled. "But remember. You promised."

There was a low laugh, then a shift in temperature as he must have sat up to remove his blindfold. My hand was picked up from the sheet and pressed to his face. I moved over it, recognizing the contours of his cheekbones, the full lips that had just been kissing me, and now a pair of closed eyes with long lashes that tickled my fingertips.

He took my hand away, and I shivered in the cool air. Almost immediately, the thighs on either side of my legs tensed, and then I felt teeth close lightly around one of my nipples.

"Beautiful," he murmured, then started trailing kisses down my abdomen. "Just fucking beautiful."

Gently, his hands removed my skirt and pushed my legs apart, and before I could respond, his mouth, warm and wet, covered my clit.

"Oh!" I cried, feeling around until I located his hair and pulled.

He grunted but didn't stop what he was doing. His mouth was working some crazy magic down there, licking, nipping, slipping in and out of me. He savored me like I was every delicacy in the world, and he needed to sample them all.

"Oh—*my*—" I was struggling for words. I wanted a name. Something to cry out when I shattered. But I had nothing, and it was the one thing I wouldn't ask of him. His identity was important to him. And I wanted his trust.

"P-*please*," I moaned. "Oh—I—Ah!"

Just when I was about to topple over the brink of absolute pleasure, he stopped what he was doing and moved back up my body, his mouth finding my navel, breast, waist, neck, and everywhere before finally reaching my lips.

"God, you taste amazing." He nuzzled just under my ear. "I could do that all damn day."

Something deep in my belly squeezed. "Why did you stop?" I wanted more. So much more.

"Because there's something else I want to do more."

A knee slipped between my thighs, urging them farther apart. And then he was back, that hard length I had sensed earlier brushing against the spaces he had just been devouring.

I shook with want.

"May I?"

I nodded, barely able to speak. "Oh-okay."

And then, as he kissed me, somehow, the kiss turned into something deeper, something more. My legs spread wider, and my hips rose, welcoming him deeper too, as slowly, slowly, he pushed inside me, one aching inch at a time.

"Oh, Christ," he muttered as his forehead landed on my shoulder. "Jesus God, Maggie, you feel fucking amazing."

My hips rocked into him, welcoming him deeper as I wove my fingers into the thick hair at the base of his neck and pulled his face back to mine for another mind-melting kiss.

"So do you," I whispered against his lips. "You feel so good."

Again, I found myself wanting that name. I wanted to shout it to the ceiling, moan it into his shoulder, shriek it to the heavens.

My stranger started to move, slowly at first, then faster as he found a rhythm that clearly worked for us both. I didn't have to do anything to help him, just kept my tight grip on his hair, holding him close. No fingers needed, no extra friction. It was only him that was necessary. My stranger. Inside me.

His teeth closed lightly around my bottom lip. I started to moan, a deep siren call set off in my belly.

"That's it," he whispered again. "Sing for me, beautiful."

He bent lower, and then I registered the feel of teeth closing around my right nipple once more. He widened his mouth, taking the whole nipple and some of my breast, worshipping me with his tongue, suckling me hard between those unbearably soft lips.

His cock thrust deeper.

I started to shake.

"Just...*please*." It seemed like the only word I was capable of.

"You can do it," my stranger told me before turning his attention to my other breast. His movements were increasingly demanding. Less forgiving. "Come for me."

"I—OH!"

My body seized and started to shake. His mouth found mine again, swallowing my cries as he drove into me with a deep insistence that commanded the orgasm pulsing through every part of me. I was coming. No, more than coming. I was jumping off that cliff, and he was right there with me.

"Fuck, *Maggie!*" he cried in between shaking, broken kisses.

I grappled for purchase, for anything to keep me from floating off this bed and dissipating into a million tiny particles. He had ruined me.

And I still didn't know his name. Or even what he looked like.

"My God," he said as his body began to relax. "You wreck me, Maggie. Do you know that?"

I reached up for my blindfold. "Can I?"

"I—"

Before he could finish his sentence, the blare of my alarm clock burst through the room. I jumped at the sudden sound. I didn't remember setting it. It was the middle of the afternoon, though a quick glance out the window told me it was morning. What had happened to the night?

The alarm grew louder and louder, making it impossible for us to relax.

Suddenly, I felt the stranger's body leave mine. I covered myself with my blanket, though I left the blindfold on. Permission. I needed his permission to take it off.

Didn't I?

"I have to go turn this thing off," he called from across the room. "It's coming from outside. Don't worry, I'll be back. We'll meet right here, okay? Just let me turn this damn thing off."

"No," I begged, reaching out blindly, trying to find his hands, his touch, anything to anchor him to me. "No, please. It's right here. Don't go yet."

"I'm sorry, I have to fix it. I have to go."

And then he was gone, though the noises persisted.

"No," I whimpered, stretching a hand out and finding nothing. "Stay. I don't even know your name."

FIFTEEN

Maggie

My phone alarm yanked me from my dream with the violence of a noose.

"No!" I cried, reaching out for a man, only to find myself staring at the popcorn ceiling of Callie's new apartment, sweat dripping down my nose while my heart raced a mile a minute.

Gradually, I sank back into the couch cushions and reminded myself again, it was just a dream.

And just like every other time, it wasn't real.

I'd been having different versions of it for the last month. Some things moved around. Sometimes we were in a hotel room, other times in the back of a club again. Once, we were in my shack on my mother's property, and another time, at a beautiful house in the mountains. But we were always blinded in some way. He always kissed me like his life depended on it. And he always disappeared before I could find out who he was.

This was the first time I'd actually dreamed about sex

with my stranger. We'd come close a few times, but usually, I woke up before anything came to fruition. This time, I was extremely conscious of the fact that I had finished in one way, at least. Calliope's orange-flowered sheets were twisted around my heaving body, and I was wrung out like a sponge —and it was only in my dreams.

I never told anyone about the stranger the night of the concert. Every time I said it out loud, only to myself, I felt ridiculous. How do you explain to someone that the best kiss you've ever experienced was with someone you've never even seen?

I went back to Irving Plaza later that night after the doors were shut. No one was there, of course. Idiot. For a week or so after the show, I haunted the venue like a ghost, just in case he really was part of the actual staff there. When that no longer made sense, given where he had been sitting and his access to the backstage area, I contacted all the bands' managers to inquire about their roadies. Nothing.

Stupid, stupid, stupid.

It was better to forget it had ever happened.

Except my brain, apparently, wouldn't let me.

On the other side of the apartment, Callie's bedside light turned on.

"You up?" she asked groggily, pulling at her silk bonnet.

I turned over the edge of the sofa and nodded. "Yeah."

She yawned, then pulled herself up. "Good. We need to meet the bus in an hour. Sound check in Burlington is at four." She swung her legs over the side of the mattress and padded into the bathroom. It wasn't until I was changed and half-packed that she sprinted out.

"Holy shit!"

I swung around. "What's the matter?"

"Look at this." She held out her phone so I could see the screen, which bore a clear headline:

Fitz Baker missing, thought lost at sea

I frowned at the screen, then back at her. "Who's that?"

She blinked at me like I was an alien. "Babe. The actor. We saw him at Irving Plaza. He was the one who started the riot, remember?"

"Ohhhh, that guy." I made a face. "He was awful."

"Well, he's gone now." Calliope swiped through the article and shook her head. "It's still sad. He was so young. Only a few years older than us, really."

She left her phone on the side table and went back to the bathroom to finish getting ready for the day. Out of morbid curiosity, I picked it up and scrolled through the rest of the article.

The U.S. Coast Guard has confirmed that the remains of a wrecked sailboat found off the coast of Maine match the one rented by actor Fitz Baker three days ago in Bar Harbor. Authorities were notified when the boat wasn't returned. The search continues along the northern coastline and neighboring Canadian islands for any sign of Baker himself, who has been missing since last Sunday.

While it's not uncommon for Baker to go off grid, as he owns a large compound in Vermont, his rep has confirmed that Baker has not been seen by anyone for nearly a week. He recently took leave from his promotional duties for *The Dwelling* in order to prioritize his mental health.

"Fitz's example is one we can all follow," said his manager, Benjamin Amaya, who also represents a number of other actors and musicians in the New York City area. "The industry has a tendency to prioritize its bottom line over the health and sanity of its artists. We should be thankful for his willingness to stand up for what's right."

Del Conte Studios, which bankrolled *The Dwelling* as well as two other Fitz Baker movies, had no comment.

Baker, who grew up sailing with his father on the Long Island Sound, was said to have spontaneously rented the boat one month after a disastrous photocall and concert at Irving Plaza in New York City. There, allegedly under the influence of unknown narcotics, he threw himself into the crowd during the show and caused a riot that sent multiple people to the hospital and for which Baker himself was arrested. It was the latest in several run-ins with the law, including a suspected drug habit and a previous breakdown at his last premiere that was captured on social media.

Baker pled guilty to three counts of attempted assault and inciting a riot in return for a community service settlement that some critics compared to a slap on the wrist. After completing two weeks' worth of *The Dwelling* press tour following his arrest, Baker bowed out to attend to his mental health.

"No one is giving up hope yet," Amaya said in a statement released yesterday. "Wherever he is, we hope Fitz knows he is loved. We'll be ready for him when he returns."

Any information regarding the disappearance of Fitz Baker should be sent to the U.S. Coast Guard's office or local authorities in Bar Harbor.

A frigid slice of eerie recognition slid down my spine as I read the article. I couldn't quite understand why I felt this way—suspicious and knowing, and also somewhat terrified. The idea of his death pounded in my chest, sort of like I'd been shoved back a step.

I frowned. I had simply brushed shoulders with this guy (if even that) before he had caused pandemonium. But it was jarring, I guess, that someone should die so young. Even more jarring because I'd met him (in a way) in person. I didn't know him. No one did, really. That's how it probably was with famous people. It must've bothered me because we'd been in such close proximity. The brush of death seemed that much more immediate.

I scrolled down a bit more to several pictures of the actor staring back at me. I remembered the *People* cover, the one where he wore a tuxedo and gleamed like a shiny new penny. His smile was bright and contagious, but his eyes were hiding something. I swiped to the next one in the gallery. This one seemed more genuine—a scowl that matched the cruel tone I'd heard that night. Lord, the man could stare a ring through a concrete wall. Those green eyes were utterly penetrating.

"You ready?"

Calliope's voice pulled me from my thoughts as she strode back into the room. I handed her back her phone, and she sighed again, then tucked it into her purse pocket.

I finished zipping up my suitcase, then started folding up the sheets.

"I'll do that."

"You don't have to go with me," I said. "You're like a mom bringing her kid to school."

"I'm a manager making sure her one and only amazing client gets where she needs to go," Callie corrected me. "Hey, look at me."

I stood up straight. As always, I felt like the dowdy one in the room. Calliope was dressed in her usual eclectic mix of color and style, while I was in my standard fare of jeans, an old T-shirt, and my favorite cardigan that nearly reached my knees. Callie had packed a whole range of stage clothes for me, and we'd been practicing ways for me to style my own hair for the last month. I was ready. But right now, I didn't feel it.

"Look at me," she said again.

I stood up straight and faced her.

"You're the shit," she said. "You're amazing. You were asked to join Gillian's tour because you killed it at your first big time show, and you're going to keep killing it. You're going to be rubbing elbows with every mover and shaker in the business, and by the end of this tour, I'm going to be fielding so many offers to sign you that we'll set records for the best deal in the last twenty years."

"But—" I started.

"But nothing," she cut me off. "That's it. That's what's going to happen. You got it?"

I opened my mouth to argue with her. To tell her about everything that could go wrong. That my stage fright might get the best of me again, or that I'd get so homesick I'd forget how to be a normal friendly person. But Callie's big eyes brooked no argument, and so I closed my mouth and nodded.

"I got it," I said. "Okay. And Callie?"

My friend smiled, like she knew what I was going to say. "I love you."

The smile widened. "I know. And I love you too, you crazy woman. Now, let's go make you famous." She picked up both of my guitars and headed for the door. "Let's start the rest of your life."

SIXTEEN

Will

I might have died for real if it hadn't been for the life jacket.

By the time I dragged myself onto the rocky beach of Boot Head Cove, an all but deserted preserve at the northern tip of Maine, waves were pounding on the shore and against the crags and cliffs. The little squall that had been threatening out there had turned into a full-fledged storm.

I couldn't have asked for better weather to fake my own death. I turned over to look out at the sea, but saw no sign of the little catamaran I'd abandoned to the ocean.

Benny and I had chosen the location carefully—about a mile offshore from Boot Head Cove, where only a handful of houses dotting the coastline could see the eight miles across to a Canadian island. Either way, the remains of the boat would be found, whether it washed up on the island or here. Either way, I'd be long gone, presumed dead.

I'd rented the cat in Bar Harbor and had made a point

to ignore their advice, say the wrong things, and generally act like a self-important prick. It was better if they thought I was an idiot. Then they'd have no problem believing I could dig my own watery grave.

And so I went, enjoying the day while the storm brewed on the horizon as I sailed the boat up the rocky Maine coastline, watching as more and more fishermen put in for the day. I spent the night moored in a tiny cove just south of Boot Head, then woke up to clouds gathering, just as predicted. And just as I jumped off the stern, the storm really hit.

Benny didn't like this part of the plan. He thought it was too easy for me to *actually* die in the stormy weather. He tried to convince me to at least hire a tugboat or something to find me on one of the little islands where the sailboat would eventually wash up. It wouldn't have worked, though. Even if by some miracle we found a captain who didn't know who I was, he would put two and two together later when the coastguard found the remains of the boat in the same area. No, the only way it would work was if I swam to shore alone and got out of Dodge as quickly as possible.

I peeled off the life preserver, silently thanking whatever part of the universe had convinced me in the end *not* to be an arrogant jackass and believe I could swim through fifteen-foot waves for a mile straight in nothing but shorts and a T-shirt. I was hopped up on adrenaline, sure. And I'd been training for the last month, open water swimming daily up and down the Long Island Sound. But looking out at the storm now, it was obvious the jacket and the wetsuit were necessary. As was a bit of luck.

A massive wave crashed onto the beach, sending spray at least ten feet into the air. My muscles were aching from fighting the water, but even with my wetsuit, I was starting to get cold. The wind was picking up, and the rain was coming down even harder as the squall made its way toward shore. I needed shelter.

Still, I sat a minute longer, watching the waves pummel the rocks.

This was it. The final moments of being Fitz Baker, if I'd ever been him at all. There was a trailhead at the end of the beach that I'd take back to the road. There, I'd find an orange pickup truck that Benny had bought for cash a few weeks ago, and inside that would be all the materials for my new life. I stared at the ocean, which was rapidly becoming a big blur.

I wanted to live.

I didn't know yet what that would look like.

But I knew I wanted to live.

"BEN, YOU ASSHOLE," I muttered as I spotted the dark orange pickup parked in a turnoff just around the next bend, about a mile from the beach.

My bare feet were numb on the wet pavement. The wind was starting to blow sideways, causing the rain to prick my face like a thousand needles.

I knew why he'd parked it here, though. Out of sight of the houses. We were going for anonymity. There would be a search for me once the boat was found, and every person who had so much as breathed in the area would be asked if they had seen me or anything strange at all. We needed that answer to be no. We needed it to be absolutely not.

The truck was nothing special either, at least twenty years old, with a little rust on the belly that wouldn't look out of place on the coast. Anyone who drove by would assume it was a fisherman's. My gut squeezed a little. It was the kind of car Dad probably would have driven had it not been for my Hollywood dollars. Now, he and Mom both had another twenty million coming their way, enough to pay for the rest of their lives and then some.

I hope they used it well. Without me.

Benny (or whoever the guy was who'd parked the truck here) had left the keys in a magnetic box over the driver's side tire. I unlocked the truck and found the necessities we'd planned: a change of clothes on the driver's seat, camping gear, and some food stowed in the back of the cab. A backpack containing several crisp stacks of cash and all the new identification in the unlikely event I'd actually need it.

"Really?" Benny had asked when I told him to put Will Baker instead of Fitzwilliam on the extremely realistic but extremely fake documents I'd need to start my new life.

I'd just snorted. "There are over four hundred thousand Bakers in the US alone, Ben. Thousands of them are named Will. No one is going to find me. And I don't want to give up my name completely."

Maybe it was naivete. Maybe I wasn't totally committed. But there was something about keeping the name my father gave me—even if just in part. A way of taking him with me without causing even more pain than I already had.

I rubbed my hand over my face. I could still see his big body rendered frail in the hospital bed. I could still see how gray his face was whenever he thought of the fact that I'd been in jail. And I could still see the expression he wore when he thought I didn't notice. It wasn't just the average shame and sorrow of any parent whose child had disappointed them. There was something else there that broke my heart. Guilt, maybe. But also acceptance. Like he knew, deep down, I'd never get any better. I'd never do anything but hurt him and everyone else around me.

I skipped the last half of the press tour for *The Dwelling*, citing my father's condition and my own mental health. Instead, I'd spent my last few weeks of being Fitz Baker at the house in Stamford, hanging out with my dad, dodging my mother's calls, and discovering who the fuck I was again without drugs or alcohol.

It cost me a lot of sleepless nights. More than a few days of losing my dinners in the upstairs toilet. But I didn't take a single pill.

Still, Dad looked at me with more shame and sorrow than ever. I came downstairs a week ago feeling like I was a new man. The withdrawals were almost gone, and for the first time in a long time, I had felt capable of something more. Wanting something more.

Dad had looked up from his coffee like he expected me to jump out a window. Like he'd given up on me, and there was nothing else he could do.

That was when I knew it was time to go.

I rubbed my face again. I'd been growing my beard for a solid month at this point, but it wasn't enough to hide my face completely. At this rate, I figured it would take six months, maybe a year, to get it to the point where people wouldn't readily recognize me. My hair even longer. I'd end up looking like a blond Sasquatch, but it was worth it for the anonymity. It was either that or go under the knife, but I couldn't quite bring myself to fuck with my face. Not yet.

Out of nowhere, I feel the soft press of Maggie's fingers framing my face.

Her touch still came to me now and then. The whisper of her fingers grazing my jaw as we kissed, or the stroke of her thumb pressing lightly into the center of my palm.

Not for the first time, I considered what might have happened that night if I had made it back to her dressing room like we'd planned. What would she have done if I'd shown her who I really was? In my worst moments, I imagined her throwing herself on me completely, picking up where we left off. I imagined her letting me strip off her clothes and having my way with her right there in that shitty little back room. I imagined bringing her to Vermont and taking her on every surface in the entire compound.

But then I imagined the telephoto lenses that would spy on us through the trees and from helicopters. I imagined the paparazzi that would stalk us from town to town, city to city, digging through her past and plastering it all over the world. I imagined the fans who would threaten her and the way that love and inspiration she had flashed from the stage would eventually burn out into nothing but smoking ash.

It was better this way.

It really was.

She was a cute girl—beautiful, in fact—but she needed my life ruining hers like she needed a hole in the head.

I smiled. If my little game had helped her on her way, if the kiss had given her the courage she needed that night, I was happy. In her own way, Maggie had given me a gift too —the knowledge that I could be liked for something other than my name or what my face might get them. That someone would want to talk to me, someone might find me interesting just for me. She'd never know it, of course. But it was the truth, nonetheless.

And that, I could take with me.

I pulled out the final item that Benny had left in the backpack: a shitty flip phone containing one text from an unfamiliar number. Benny on another burner. We had an agreement; text to confirm I'd made it, and then we'd both get rid of the phones and confine our communication to anonymous letters. Phone records could be subpoenaed in case someone (read: my mother) ever suspected anything. Letters could be burned.

I opened the phone and found the message wasn't a text at all, but a link. I clicked on it and waited while the phone's crappy browser eventually led to an article from a local paper in Boston reviewing a concert.

Gillian Jacobs & Co set to smash at the Sentinel!

The article was a rave review of Gillian Jacobs's latest album and an excited announcement for her next show. At the top, there was a picture of the band along with the other musicians joining her tour.

She would have been easy to miss. Near the edge of the photo, Maggie wore a green dress this time that came just past her knees but had on the same boots she'd worn that night at Irving Plaza. Her hair was tamed into a bun at the top of her head, and her eyes were lined in black, flashing with excitement even in this tiny photo. She was shying from the camera, looking mostly like she thought she was in the wrong place. But she wanted to be there. Anyone could see that.

Again, I felt that touch on my lips.

"Maggie," I murmured, enjoying the way her name felt on my tongue.

I scanned the article, eventually coming to a short paragraph about her.

Perhaps most surprising is the addition of unsigned newcomer Maggie Sharp, whose cool sound recalls the traditional styling of Emmylou Harris while embodying a soul sound you can't find anywhere in country. Her self-produced EP is excellent, if a little unpolished. She's sure to get snatched up by a label by the end of the tour. We'll be watching this star in the making and picking up her album whenever it drops.

I smirked. Benny knew what he was doing sending me this article. Burlington was maybe two hours from my compound, which I decided to leave to my parents. He knew I was planning to drive that way anyway, go around the big cities, and camp until I could get out of the Northeast and had enough facial hair to avoid recognition. He was hoping the temptation of seeing The Girl, as he called her, would be too much, and I'd back out of this insane plan.

Well, I wasn't. If anything, being sober made me that much more intent on my purpose. Disappear. The world would forget Fitz Baker after enough time had passed. This girl had no idea what was coming if fame chose her. If that was actually what she wanted. But her music was brilliant. I knew that firsthand. I wasn't going to get in her way.

I exited the browser and pulled up Benny's message to punch in my response.

Me: At the truck.

Benny: Oh good, you're alive.

I chuckled. He was playing it cool, but he was worried about me. It felt kind of good.

Me: Barely. But I made it. What's with the link?

His reply came quickly.

Benny: Consider it a reminder of what's out there if you change your mind. She's waiting for you.

I swallowed. Benny always could read me better than anyone else.

Me: No changing. I'm ready to go.

Benny: You want to be rescued, you know who to call.

I stared at the message for a long time, then sighed and typed out my answer.

Me: I'll let you know where I land. Thanks, man.

Benny: Anytime, brother.

My thumb hovered over the send button for a minute longer. And then, finally, I pressed it, powered off the phone, then drove back to the beach, and threw it into the water.

Maybe it was extreme, but we had an agreement. Get rid of the evidence. Get rid of my life.

I pulled on my cap and tugged my raincoat close, oblivious to the storm, while I stared out at the waves one last time, lost in the hypnotic gray, the places where the horizon and the ocean blended together and no separation existed between sky and earth. Then I walked back to the truck, got in, and drove away, acutely aware that for the first time in my entire life, I really was completely and totally alone.

EPILOGUE

Will

"Goddammit."

The truck came to a creaky stop, brakes shouting and oil gauge clicking just before I turned off the engine. There was no getting around it. The brake pads were shot after putting at least thirty thousand miles on this beat-up piece of garbage over the last six months.

Since leaving the rocky coast of Maine, I'd zigzagged my way through the northern part of the United States, sticking mostly to logging roads and Forest Service campgrounds, stopping only to replenish supplies while wearing the wig and prosthetic nose that kept people from looking too closely.

Right now, though, it looked like the north side of Rainier would have to wait.

I flipped down the visor and examined my reflection in the mirror. Six months had done a lot, that was for sure. Between constant outdoor activity and a steady diet of fresh foods minus the constant supply of drugs fucking up my immune system, I was probably healthier now than I'd ever been in my life. Shock, I know. No more dark circles under my eyes or hollowed cheeks. My skin color wasn't that fake orange the studios painted on me anymore, but a healthy, ruddy tan that only came from spending a lot of time outdoors. And my hair was growing long and full instead of in stringy patches.

Healthy looked good. Who knew?

I tugged at my beard, still unaccustomed to this appearance. I'd had a beard before, but never like this one, a scraggly blond mess that nearly reached my collarbone, completely obscuring my jawline and mouth. It was a damn mess and needed a trim, but it had finally gotten to the point where it hid just about every recognizable feature I had.

I pulled out the tie holding my hair back, and the messy waves fell to my shoulders. So that the only thing left from my previous life was my father's long, straight nose and my mother's green eyes—that damn bright green that more than one outlet had termed my "stargazers."

Just like it always did, the thought of my parents, especially my dad, caused that knot in my stomach to tighten. When I'd last spoken with Benny—a burner phone conversation about two weeks ago—he'd confirmed that everyone was doing all right. Dad was healthy. Mom was...Mom. Occasionally, one of them would be interviewed about my disappearance, but the search had been called off long ago. A memorial had taken place. People were moving on.

I did wonder sometimes if forcing my parents to mourn their son was the best way to go. But I knew my family. We were stuck, all of us, in this vicious cycle of fame and distance that would have only continued if I'd stuck around. We fed off each other's unhappiness. The only way out was with my exit. And the only way either one of them would accept that was if they thought I was dead.

I exhaled with those memories and refocused on figuring out where the hell I was. The Thomas Guide informed me I was closer to civilization than I thought, on a lakeside road north of State Highway 5 on the Idaho-Washington border. Yes, I had learned to use an old-fashioned atlas to take me through most of the northern US. That's what you do when you stubbornly avoid people for half a year and refuse to get a new cell phone because you've had others tapped too many times by the paparazzi.

Oddly, the paranoia that life in the spotlight had inspired had gotten even worse now that I was out of it. But when you're enjoying a bit of anonymity for the first time in your life, you become really scared to lose it. Six months into this strange odyssey, I knew one thing: there was no fucking way I could ever be Fitz Baker again.

Right now, though, I was sure of something else: my truck needed fixing. And I was actually going to have to speak to someone to get it done.

I peered through my ice-crusted windshield at one of the smallest gas stations I'd ever seen—if you could even call it that. The log-cabin-styled A-frame building boasted a single pump near its back, accessible through a small path in the grass and facing what looked like a frozen lake. Across the top of a rickety front door was a crooked sign that read General Store, and a neon Open in the window with the *p* blinking its last life alongside a dancing Santa Claus and some twinkle lights around the sill.

That's right, it was Christmas. Maybe a few days before, if I had counted correctly. Mom would make her yearly trip back to Connecticut, where she and Dad would pull out the old stockings my grandmother had knitted everyone when I was just a baby. Dad would drink hot buttered rums and watch football; Mom would talk on the phone while she made peppermint cookies for the neighbors.

Or maybe they wouldn't this year. Maybe that was all just a dream they tried to live once a year for me. We were never the warmest of families, but we did have some traditions. Didn't we?

Suddenly, the idea of being alone in the woods sounded more like a sentence than a refuge. Remnants of snow were still on the ground, with more flakes threatening above.

And I had no idea where I was going to set up camp for the night.

The door to the little log A-frame swung open and closed with a loud rap, yanking me from my thoughts. A man wearing a brown hunting jacket and a worn baseball cap strode out, passing my truck with a brief glance. He was probably my age and had the same profile I'd seen countless times across the country: pale skin, dull eyes, shoulders older than his age, and beefy hands that could handle a tractor or a shovel.

"Lucas!"

The man turned around toward a middle-aged woman with a mop of gray hair and a friendly, birdlike face who was poking her head out of the store.

"You forgot your eggs, honey," she said, handing him a paper bag over the edge of the wood railing.

The man took it gratefully. "Thanks, Kathy. Yeah, Mom would have my guts if I forgot them. Hey, listen." He pulled a worn leather wallet from his pocket, extracted a bill, and handed it to the woman. "Put this toward Ellie's tab, will you?"

The woman looked confused as she took the fifty. "You

sure, hon? You know she's only going to spend her extra money at the bar."

"Well, don't sell her anything yourself," Lucas said. "Just...for Maggie's sake, you know?"

Kathy seemed hesitant but pocketed the money anyway. "Have you heard from her lately?"

Lucas shook his head. "Not since she left the last time. That was, what, two and a half years ago? She told me she wasn't coming back until her mom is sober. So maybe never?" He shrugged. "If I can help, I will."

"Sweet boy." Kathy patted him on the face. "You say hi to your mom for me."

"Will do." Lucas glanced toward me. "I'll be going. You've got another customer."

Kathy looked over his shoulders, curiosity apparent in her eyes when she found me. "Well, you coming in, hon?" she called. "You look to be freezing out there."

That was apparently my cue. I waited until his car—another truck, of course—had pulled away before I got out of mine and followed the woman into the little store. The store itself was nothing special. A few rows of basic sundries, a line of refrigerators in the back holding drinks, bait, and some other random things, and a counter near the front where they seemed to sell anything from frozen pizzas to "mocha lattes." And, apparently, cheap beer from a keg under the counter.

"Bad news, Ellie," Kathy said to a woman at the counter. "Keg's all tapped out."

The woman turned. She was tall—almost as tall as me—and skinny, clothed in ill-fitting jeans and a men's parka that was at least two sizes too big. She had curly light brown hair that looked like it hadn't been brushed in a while and the red-tipped nose of someone who drank too much. A boozehound, then. So that's where Kathy thought that Lucas guy's money would go. She was probably right, too. I would know.

"You're holding out on me, Kathy Tibbs," Ellie snapped as Kathy approached. "I know you got a new keg yesterday. You always get them on Tuesdays."

I took a right to examine a selection of bait behind one refrigerated door. Maybe I should have stayed in the car.

"Ellie, calm down now," Kathy cooed as she returned behind the register. "You've had enough today, and I can smell it from here. Now, why don't you take the rest of these groceries home—on me, if you want—and just cool off. You'll feel better for it in the morning."

I selected a soda and a bag of chips and cautiously made my way toward the counter.

"Fine," hissed Ellie. "But don't you be thinking you're better than me. Don't you dare!"

She whirled around with her small selection of groceries, pushing past me with enough vigor that she didn't notice when something fluttered from her purse.

"Ah, ma'am?"

The word sounded odd. I wasn't sure I'd ever addressed anyone that way. Usually, I was the one whose ass people were kissing. But you learned things on the road. Things people in the city, or at least in the odd, narcissistic world I had left, seemed to have forgotten. Things like basic fucking manners.

"What?"

I picked up the paper from the floor and held it out when she turned. "You dropped this."

Ellie snatched the photo from my hand. "Oh, her." Contempt dripped through her slurred voice. "That's *Maggie*. That's my no-good daughter. Moved away.

Thinks she's better than us too, you know. Just like Kathy here."

"Now, Ellie..."

The name sent a shiver down my arm while the two women bickered. Ellie set it down on the counter so she could really lean into the fight. That was when I got a look. And about fainted.

No, it couldn't be. How many Maggies were there in the United States? A million? Two?

The child in the posed school photo couldn't have been more than eight years old, with the rounded cheeks of someone who hadn't quite found her bones yet. But her smile, the soulful brown eyes, unruly black-brown hair was all familiar. Wasn't it? Or was I just fooling myself, after six months of being on my own, that this child had grown up to be a stranger I'd met through a silk screen?

Impossible.

"Does she ever come back?" I asked, trying for casual but clearly failing miserably.

Ellie's face curled up in a snarl when she turned her attention back to me. "Like her, do you?"

I backed up, holding my hands out. "I was just wondering. You seemed to miss her."

Ellie glared at me, like she was trying to figure something out, her dark eyes darting up and down, taking in my beard, my face, my old jeans, even the hat. I tried my best not to move. Not to look like someone who couldn't deal with a few mild questions. Not to look guilty.

"She'll never come back," she bit out. "Not that it's any business of a stranger."

And then, before I could answer, she rushed out of the store, letting the door bang closed behind her as she left.

"Sorry about that, hon," Kathy said as I approached the

counter. "That's just Ellie. You don't need to pay her any attention to her. Ellie just has a bit too much drink sometimes, you know?"

I nodded. She had no idea.

"What did you say your name is, hon?" asked Kathy while she rang up my items.

I pulled the bill of my cap down low. "Ah, Will. Just Will."

"Well, Just Will, that'll be four thirty-two for the soda and chips. Need anything else?"

Zero recognition gleamed in her eyes. Just mild curiosity and a bit of concern.

So I made a choice.

"Actually, yeah," I told her while handing over the cash. "My brakes are shot. I was hoping someone around here could help me out so I can get back on the road."

Kathy shook her head with regret. "Sorry, hon. We don't have a repair shop here. My husband could probably change your oil for you, but that's about it. Craig Somner, though, he fixes cars in the back of his barn, about two miles west toward the highway. If you want, I can give him a call, and he can probably give you a tow too once the road gets plowed."

We both looked dubiously at the barely paved, two-lane road I'd practically slid down. It wasn't bad—I'd driven a lot worse, especially up near the border. But winter was definitely here, and a town like this was last on the list for utilities. I needed a place to stay, somewhere to get out of the cold. And not just for the night but for the foreseeable future.

Still, I couldn't figure that out until I had a working vehicle.

"A tow would be great," I said. "I'm not in a hurry."

"Good, hon. You need a place to stay? We rent out the trailer in the back for folks who need it. You wouldn't be the first one to get stranded in the snow, that's for sure."

I nodded. I could have said no. I could have pulled my tent out of the truck, hiked into the woods, and spent the night out there, just like I had been doing for months.

But instead, I found I wanted to take this stranger up on her offer.

"Sure," I said. "That would be great."

Kathy nodded happily, oblivious to my inner conflict.

I glanced outside again. "You don't have a payphone around, do you? I need to check in with someone, and I lost my cell."

I needed to call Benny to get things squared away for the car—even to get a new one if I had to. I wasn't about to use this woman's phone to do it.

Kathy shook her head while she organized receipts. If she wondered why I wasn't requesting to use the store's phone, she didn't ask. "No, but Bob—that's my husband—will be back in, oh, a few hours. He just headed into town, and I know he's stopping at Fred Meyer. Want me to ask if he can pick up one of those preloaded phones for you?"

Relieved I didn't have to explain the concept of a burner phone or make up an excuse for why I needed one, I just nodded. "That would be great, thanks."

"You got it. I'll need a few hours to get the trailer ready for you, but you're welcome to wait in here if you like."

"Actually, I think I'll take a walk," I said.

Again, Kathy surprised me by just nodding. "Might as well before the next storm comes. We've got snowshoes to rent in the corner."

I declined the shoes, but said thank you regardless, then quickly packed up to explore the lake.

ABOUT TWO HOURS LATER, I'd walked half the perimeter of the lake. It was bigger than I thought, curving around a lot of smaller inlets despite hilly rises and steep descents. Pine trees covered most of the terrain, hiding a lot of the small vacation rentals and cabins from plain sight. I was passed by maybe two cars, despite the fact that it wasn't even noon. Occasionally, I'd hear the rumble of a generator or the roar of a snowblower. But for the most part, I was surrounded by quiet in the blanket of leftover snow and ice.

There was something about this place, I realized as I continued my walk. Something familiar. Maybe it really was because I liked it. Maybe it was just because I was ready to stay put for a while after being on the self-imposed lam for six months. But I felt comfortable here. I found myself wondering if I could actually find a house or something where I could be without anyone bothering me. With running water. And a bed that wasn't on the ground.

As if in answer to my question, I rounded the corner to find a for-sale sign tipping crookedly out from the side of the road. Over the top of the sign, in large red letters, read: Lakefront Cabin.

"No shit," I murmured, then looked around. "Now, where the hell is the damn place?"

I almost couldn't find the driveway, which was so narrow it was practically a deer path leading from the main road down a rocky hillside to nowhere. Maybe it was just a piece of property, then. Not the worst thing, but not the best thing. Building a house wasn't insurmountable. It would just take time.

Then the drive turned, and I was faced with a small lodge built directly into the hillside, surrounded by pines.

Down the hill, the lake gleamed like a facet of crystal. But on either side of the little house, there were no signs of the neighbors I knew must be there. Between the thickets of brush, salal, and columns of trees, the forest was too dense.

The house itself was obviously vacant, and probably had been for years, if not decades. Three of the four windows were boarded up. The wood siding was streaked with moss, and the roof looked like it was about to fall in.

It was perfect.

I wandered about the property a bit more, scrambling down the hill to the water, where a decrepit old dock stretched out into the icy glass. Across the lake, I could see houses dotting the lakeside. There were a few to the left and right of this property, but they were far enough that they looked more like Tic Tacs than actual buildings. The property was big. Too big for one person, really, which was probably why it was for sale.

I made my way back up to the main road to get the information for the realtor and was confronted by another sign across the street, on the side of the road that led directly up the mountain that looked over the entire lake. This one was nearly as tall as I was, with big block letters across the front.

For sale: 150 acres.

Within seconds, I could imagine everything. Well. Septic. A solar array for the house. A team could demo the interior, renovate everything, maybe add another floor at the bottom. I didn't need a mansion here. Just a few rooms to myself. A refuge where no one could find me. That's it. A place to land when I wanted to stop moving.

I'd felt glimmers of peace in my life before. It didn't happen often. Several times over the last six months, usually when I was listening to the birds in the morning from inside my tent or when I watched the sun set over a particularly beautiful meadow.

And with her, yeah. Maggie.

I shook my head. Even that name was fading, right along with the rest of that life. I thought of her from time to time, of course. Usually at night. Usually, when I was so desperate for a touch, I couldn't help but do it myself.

But after, I tucked the memories of her fingers, her voice, and her sweet mouth away, because, like everything else, I had to let her go. Even the peace I'd had at that moment. I couldn't chase any of it anymore.

And yet, here it was. I'd never see Maggie or anyone else from that life, but maybe in this new one, I'd meet someone who made me feel that way again. Someone who could share this place with me. Someone I could trust.

In the meantime, I'd carve out this small sanctuary of my own and bide my time.

I didn't know how long everything would take. Years? Hopefully not. Months, fine. Time was all I had. Benny would handle it—God knew I was paying him enough, although he'd do it out of friendship, regardless. He'd know what to do. How to buy the land and the house so that no one would know. How to arrange for designers, contractors, engineers, anyone else that was needed without involving me.

I turned on my heel, eager to return to the store. I needed to call Benny.

I needed to start my life.

Thank you for reading Hollywood Touch, prequel to the Discreet duet!

If you haven't already, continue reading Will and Maggie's story with Hollywood Secret, where our lovers reconnect!

Read here: www.nicolefrenchromance.com/ hollywoodsecret

Keep reading for the first few chapters of their story.

FROM HOLLYWOOD SECRET

Maggie

"It all needs a lot of work, Mama. I don't know how else to say it."

I plopped into one of the chairs on the front lawn and handed Mama a bottle of water, hoping to temper the rum and Coke she was already nursing after work today. I took a long drink from my own bottle and used the bottom of my stained t-shirt to wipe sweat off my brow. Before sweeping and collecting dried pine needles around the cottages, I finished reviewing the list of Mama's maintenance requests and had made a list of my own. If she was serious about turning this place into a B&B, there was so, so much to be done. But for some reason, the looks on Cathy's and Lucas's faces just made me that much more determined to help her do it.

The water bottle toppled over on the grass while Mama took a long sip of her drink. She grimaced and shook her head, her bangs bouncing slightly. "Don't sugarcoat it, Maggie Mae. Lay it on me now."

I sighed. Over the last few days, I'd been combing through all of the requirements needed to get this business off the ground, and Lucas had come by earlier to walk around the property with me, doing an informal inspection. Mama's pet project had morphed into my crusade.

"You and Alan did some nice cosmetic stuff on the property with the paint and the landscaping. But the two outer cottages need new plumbing since last winter's freeze, and they both look like they have some pretty bad flood damage from the spring flooding that will probably require us to replace the drywall completely. All three houses need new roofs, but maybe we can get away with some patching. I don't know. On top of that, if you want to get licensed, there are a bunch of things that have to be done to the stairs, to the electric and heating systems, all in order to get the place up to code."

I looked to Mama, who sipped nervously on her cocktail. I knew what she was thinking. Repairs meant money, and money was what neither of us had at the moment.

"This is beyond me, Mama," I admitted. "I can paint and clean. Some minor landscaping, help with the livestock. But these are major infrastructural problems. You need someone who can help you with this stuff now, even if we don't try for the B&B thing."

"And with what money am I supposed to do that, Margaret?" she bit out. She stared angrily out at the lake, refusing to meet my imploring gaze.

"Mom," I said gently. "We'll figure it out."

I didn't know what else to say. She didn't move, likely hearing the uncertainty in my voice. I reached out and touched her arm gently, causing her to look down at my fingers on her freckled forearm. When she finally looked back up, her eyes shone angrily with a fine gloss of tears. Tears and drink. Always drink.

I removed my hand.

"That goddamn bastard," she muttered fiercely. "Left me in this mess. We sunk everything into this place, Maggie. *Everything*. I've got nothing left. Do you understand that?"

I didn't have to answer. I'd seen the state of her finances. She had liquidated her entire 401k in order to finance the remodel on the property, all wasted through Alan's bad investment schemes and debt maneuvering. Just before he left, Mama filed bankruptcy. This property was all she had left, and only because it was her home.

She looked back at the lake, taking deep breaths. She slid the sunglasses resting on her head down over her eyes, masking her emotions while she drained the rest of her glass. I stood up, sensing her need to be alone. You couldn't talk to her when she was like this, though I'd almost certainly be picking her up off the couch in another few hours.

"I'm going to go for a run," I said. "I'll take a quick look in the storage shack to see if there is anything worth selling on my way up to the road." It was a feeble attempt to make things right, but I already knew I'd be calling Lucas tomorrow. So much for independence.

"There's not," Mama snapped. "But you take your time. Take the whole evening if you need. Honestly, Maggie, I just want to be alone without you bothering me for once."

I tried not to let her words hurt, though the sharpness in her voice reminded me of why I left in the first place. And just how much worse it could get.

"I'll look anyway," I said quietly. Then I patted her on the shoulder and left.

It turned out that Mama was right—all that was left in storage were boxes of yard sale knickknacks, my childhood paraphernalia, and a few pieces of miscellaneous furniture and other odds and ends. Certainly nothing of monetary value.

But if I was being honest, that wasn't what I was looking for anyway. I found those things right away: a bag of the gear I once used to swim laps across the lake in the early morning, and my old bike, resting in the back next to a pump. Nothing was too out of shape. The swimmer's buoys just needed to be pumped up, and the bike, though definitely in need of a tune-up, still seemed rideable. Thinking vaguely of the triathlon flyer, I decided a ride sounded better than a run. I used to cycle the hilly twenty-eight miles around the lake on a regular basis. If I could still do it now, maybe doing a triathlon wasn't so far-fetched. And I couldn't ask for a better distraction.

After pumping up the tires, I wheeled the bike up to the road. Some cloud cover had finally settled across the skies after almost a week of sweat-inducing sunshine. I turned left down the backside of the hill, basking in the peace of the lake and a sense of freedom I hadn't felt in years.

Come back soon, Flower.

It was what he always said anytime I left him. For a walk. A run. A gig. A job. In the time we lived together, I had stopped running or doing anything outside completely, locked instead in his lavish apartment. I was lucky if I found an hour a week to myself, let alone an afternoon to do what I wanted. He so intensely resented anything outside of our life together that gradually, I gave up almost everything that mattered to me to make him happy. Everything except music, and for that most of all, he had punished me. A slap here. A shout there. And eventually, so much worse. Still I had taken it, having been convinced for most of my life that I was never enough.

I coasted down the hill, feeling that knot in my stomach release just a bit more, continuing even when I started to pedal uphill and felt a long unfamiliar burn in my thighs. *Go!* I thought fiercely. This was my time. I didn't want to waste it.

For most of the ride, I did all right. I had to stop around mile eight to walk the bike up one nasty hill, but from there, I rode another ten, huffing and puffing up the smaller hills in order to fly down again, the comforting smell of dry pine needles and briny lake water filling my nose as I went.

Unfortunately, it was in the middle of one long coast with my eyes partially shut that I missed a massive pothole. It pitched me off my bike and down another steep hillside. I rolled about twenty feet through the soft, needle-covered forest floor until I hit the base of a large pine tree with a thump that made me see stars.

I lay there for a second and focused on breathing in and out with the wind. Could I move my fingers and toes? The answer was yes—okay, I wasn't dead or paralyzed. I sucked in another large breath and sat up slowly, feeling the side of my head that had smacked the dirt and gravel. There was only a slight scrape, although I'd definitely have a bump there later. I didn't *think* I had a concussion. And shockingly, I didn't appear to have any other major scrapes and bruises—just an unholy amount of pine needles and dirt clinging to my bike shorts and shirt.

I looked up the hill to where my bike lay innocuously on its side.

"You little shit," I denounced it.

There was nothing to do but get up and ride home. All nine-plus miles there. But when I tried to push myself up, a shooting pain lanced through my right ankle, and immediately, I yowled and fell right back on my ass, sliding a few more feet down the hill.

"Fuck!" I cried, clasping the offended body part. "Shit! You fucker!" I yelled at the bike, now more than a little annoyed with it.

Slowly, I managed to pull myself up onto one leg next to a tree. I looked down the hill, hoping to find a house or a cabin or *someplace* to find help. I didn't know many people on this side of the lake, although there had been rumors of a clan of skinheads since I was a kid (not that I've ever seen any). Even though neighboring Idaho supposedly had a fairly large white power community, I'd always thought there were more likely meth labs than Neo-Nazis. Still, considering my skin was a few shades darker than most folks around here, and I had the notoriety of being Ellie Sharp's bastard kid, I wasn't interested in taking my chances.

"Great," I muttered. "Now I'm going to be whacked by Walter White."

"There are worse ways to go."

At the sudden deep, male voice behind me, I screamed and jumped onto my bad leg, falling again and rolling another three feet down the hill. I scrambled back up, ignoring the pinches around my ankle and calf, then grabbed another tree trunk, looked up, and froze. There he was: a real, live yeti.

Well, not quite. Upon closer inspection, it was a man, but only just. He was tall—at least six feet, more likely six-two or six-three. Dressed in grungy cargo pants and a t-shirt that looked like it had more holes than fabric, his tan, sinewy limbs filled out hole-ridden cotton better than it deserved, revealing muscles that looked more like the product of natural hard work than hours spent in a gym.

His hair was a wild riot of dark blond that, when combined with a severely unkempt beard that extended well past his collar, made him strongly resemble a lion. And yet, even in the midst of this wild man's ferocious appearance, a pair of equally wild green eyes looked just the slightest bit familiar. Did I know him from somewhere? Maybe an old high school classmate, or someone who used to hang around Lucas's crowd from before. I squinted, trying to place him.

His mouth, wide and full, twitched. He tilted his head, and something in me clicked, like a lock that had just been picked.

Gorgeous.

The word echoed through my head before I could even think consciously.

Wait, *what?*

The man shuffled down the hill, then reached out a hand. Slowly, I took it, though I gasped at the warmth of his grip, apparent even in the early evening sunshine. His hand was broad, practically a paw, and slightly calloused across his palm and fingertips. This was someone who spent his days using his body, not sitting indoors.

He jerked at the contact too, like he'd been shocked. His squeeze tightened, and I allowed him to guide me toward the road.

"I—uh—thanks," I stuttered, hopping toward him on one foot and nearly losing my balance again.

He didn't answer, just cast a look over at my hobbling form, pulled my hand around his neck, and slung an arm around my waist before lifting me completely off the ground, effectively carrying me the rest of the way up the hill. I might have protested more if I hadn't been one hundred percent entranced by the solid wall of *man* pressed against me, feeling intoxicatingly...good. Because *God*, did he smell good.

Like rain. That's what it was. Soap, of course, and a bit of sweat—he had clearly been in the middle of some kind of workout when he'd seen me fall down the hill. But through all of that was a fresh, vibrant scent, the kind I used to crave when I was stuck in the city for weeks at a time. The kind that would make me run up to the roof of my building when summer thunderstorms hit Manhattan, or make me stop on the side of the road when I'd cross the unlikely bay or river driving between gigs. He smelled like water. Briny. A little sweet. Unbelievably fresh and potent.

It wasn't until he set me down next to the fairly unkempt dirt road that I realized we weren't just stuck in the woods. We were obviously on someone's property—*his* property, if the narrow driveway, the beat-up Toyota pickup, and the battered wood cabin were any indicators.

"There," he said, stepping a solid three feet away, almost as if he couldn't stand to be next to me. He wrinkled his nose. It only then occurred to me that after an eighteen-mile bike ride, I probably reeked. Fantastic. Mountain man was all delectable fresh water, and I probably smelled like a shoe.

"You all right now?" he asked. "Those pine needles are slick."

I had to physically fight the urge not to step back toward him to answer. What the hell was wrong with me?

"Um, y-yeah," I managed, unable to cover my stammer. "I'm f-fine."

His gaze dragged over me. In the sunlight, his green eyes were clearly flecked with gold. We stared at each other, letting the sounds of the wind in the trees and the cry of the osprey fill the space between us. My heart thumped. A vein in the man's temple twitched.

"So, um, thank you..." I ventured, waiting for him to fill in his name. I extended a hand, telling myself it was the polite thing to do, not because I wanted to touch him again.

But the man only stared at it, then shoved a hand into his wild hair and looked back up at me like I'd just offered him a handful of stinging nettles.

"Do you need a ride home?" he asked abruptly.

"I, uh, it's okay, I can just—" I took a step backward, and immediately, my ankle buckled. Shit. I could stand on it, but the idea of riding nine miles home sounded like pure torture.

Goldilocks (as he had become the second he refused to tell me his name) glared at my ankle like it had personally offended him. I glared back. He blinked.

"Let me grab my keys," he grumbled and jogged down the hill into the house, returning a few moments later. "Come on," he said, and before I could reply, squatted down and scooped me into his arms, dangling my feet over one elbow.

Damn. That smell. It really was even better up close.

"Here." Goldilocks dumped me unceremoniously into the passenger seat of his burnt-orange pickup, then dusted off his hands, like he was trying to get rid of all traces of me.

He paused, one hand on the door while he watched me situate myself. When I looked up, his penetrating green gaze practically bore through me.

"What?" I asked, suddenly picking at my hair. God, I probably still had pine needles everywhere. We were quite a pair. Yeti-locks and the pine needle bear. Awesome.

The stranger jerked, as if pulled out of a trance, then

folded his mouth into a thin, tight line. "Nothing," he snapped and shut the door in my face.

I sat awkwardly as he walked around the car, got in, and started it up. The windows were down and the old engine was loud, but that did nothing to distract from the immediacy of his scent crowding me in the small cab. Rainwater, yeah. And something else, something sweet. Caramel? Chocolate?

I wasn't ready to think about just why I was so interested.

"Um, that's my bike on the road," I pointed out as he backed past the old Schwinn lying in a heap by the potholes.

Goldilocks rolled his lips together, cast his eyes upward like he was searching for patience, and stopped the car to throw the bike in the back.

"Your tires look like shit," he remarked once he got back in and started driving. "No wonder you crashed. They are completely bald."

"They were fine until I hit that pothole up there. The bigger problem is probably that I had my eyes shut."

At that, his full mouth twitched again. This time it was definitely noticeable.

"You were riding with your eyes shut?"

I blushed. "Only for a second. Don't you ever get that feeling when you're just kind of caught up in how good something feels? I was coasting, and the wind was blowing, and it just felt *awesome.*" I sighed, and giggled to myself. "Well, until I toppled down the hill and busted my ankle. But before that I felt...free."

"Free," he repeated quietly. The thrum of his voice filled the car, and almost matched the engine.

We passed more than half the drive around the lake

without saying anything beyond me giving directions and him grunting in response. Either the radio didn't work, or the guy wasn't feeling music. But I wasn't the kind of person who could sit easily in silence.

"So, um, I haven't seen you around. Have you lived on the lake long?"

He darted a side-eyed green look at me. "A few years."

I ventured a smile. Okay, he was talking. "Where were you from originally?"

Another suspicious glance. Jesus, the guy could seriously break glass with his intensity. "Connecticut."

"Connecticut, really? You're a long way from home. What brought you all the way to Newman Lake?"

He worried his jaw for a minute, and a gust of wind through the window caused his beard to wave slightly. I didn't even like facial hair on men—it obscured the face, not to mention made it scratchy when you kissed—but this guy, those eyes. I swear, I could barely see anything past them.

"I just wanted a change of pace," he said finally, gripping the steering wheel so hard his knuckles turned white.

I nodded. "I get that. That's why I'm back myself, I suppose. I was actually living in New York for the last eight years, believe it or not. But I grew up here, so this is home, I guess. I'm Maggie, by the way. You, um, you actually look kind of familiar. Are you sure we haven't met before, maybe back in the cit—"

"We don't need to do that," he cut in abruptly.

I recoiled against the force of his voice. "Don't need to do what? Turn left here, by the way."

His eyes remained steadfast on the road as he turned onto West Newman Lake Road. "The whole getting to know you thing. 'What's your name, where're you from, blah, blah, blah.' I don't give a shit who you are, and that's all you need to know about me. I'm taking you home because it was the quickest way to get you the hell off my property."

Then he finally did look at me again, and his expression sliced like a knife. Everything about him seemed etched by a razor: the long line of his nose, the chiseled edges of his muscles, the angles of his bent knees and elbows. There was nothing soft about this man. He was sharp. Feral.

I flinched. I couldn't help it. His eyes flickered over me with something I might have confused with concern if I didn't already know what a dick he was.

"Hey," he started. "Ah—Maggie. I—"

"It's fine," I said, hating how small my voice had become. I crossed my arms and wrapped my hands over my shoulders, hugging myself. I had already lived with someone who treated me like shit. I wasn't interested in putting up with it from complete strangers, ride home or not. "You can pull over at the sign right there."

"It's all right, I'll just drive you down to the—"

"It's *fine*," I said again. "Just pull over."

He opened his mouth like he wanted to say something more, then sighed and did as I asked. I hopped out while he pulled my bike down from the bed. I took it and wheeled it to the curb, limping on one foot. The pain was already better, but I'd be exclusively swimming for at least a week if I still wanted to compete next month.

"You all right?"

When I turned around, Goldilocks was back in the driver's seat, his door still open as he watched my progress. One long, muscled leg balanced on the ground. I parked the bike, then hopped back over to him as defiantly as I could.

"I'm the hell off your property now," I told him evenly. "So we don't have to do this. Thanks for the ride."

Before he could reply, draw me back in with those hypnotic green eyes and that scent that made me forget where I was, I shut the car door in the stranger's face. Eager to return to the house that, for all its faults, never left me feeling as disoriented and confused as I'd been for the past twenty minutes.

Keep reading all of Will and Maggie's story here: www.nicolefrenchromance.com/ hollywoodsecret

AFTERWORD

Whenever people ask me what my best book is, I always answer the same: the Discreet duet. The series never did quite as "well" as some of my more popular and typical trilogies. It doesn't quite have the same kinds of tropes or backgrounds readers have come to expect from my work.

Maybe that's because this story was written for my own heart. Maybe that's why I think it's the best romance series I've written to date.

The prequel for this series has been half written for years, mostly because I needed to know: what would actually drive a person to abandon their life, to the point of faking their own death? What kind of misery would you have to be in to believe the people around you would genuinely be better off if you no longer existed in their lives?

To be extraordinarily clear: what Will did is wrong. Deceiving others about your death or anyone else's diminishes the very real suffering of suicidal thoughts and the extraordinary pain of losing someone you know and care about in that way.

If you or anyone else you know struggles with suicide, self-harm, or or addiction, there are many resources available to help. Start by visiting https://988lifeline.org/ to learn more.

XO,
Nicole French

ACKNOWLEDGMENTS

This story has been in the works for years, but wouldn't have been possible without the unending support and patience of the following people:

First, my husband and kids, who deal with the idiosyncrasies of a hare-brained writer and somehow still manage to love her anyway. I am grateful daily for that.

Second, to my team of alpha readers, Patricia, Dawn, and Danielle (also my assistant), whose utter love of Will encouraged me to continue his story even when, to be honest, he seemed like an unbearable jerk. You are such blessings!

Thirdly, to the wonderful professionals behind every Nicole French release: Dani Sanchez at Wildfire Marketing, editor Emily Hainsworth, and proofreader Marla Esposito all work tirelessly to ensure each book is its best. Thank you!

Fourthly, and perhaps most importantly: every single reader, new and old, who take the time to read my work. I am endlessly grateful for you. You make it possible for me to tell stories for a living. I could not do this without you. THANK YOU.